MURDER ON VACATION

Molly Sutton Mysteries 6

NELL GODDIN

Beignet Books

ISBN: 978-1-949841-06-0

For my generous father, C. Hobson Goddin, for sticking with me even when he thinks I am nuts.

CONTENTS

I

2007

The second week of February, cold and damp. Molly Sutton stood looking out the French doors of *La Baraque* at the frosty landscape, struggling with the feeling that she should be a lot happier than she was.

After all, her move to France had turned out even better than her wildest dreams: she loved her village, had good friends, and enjoyed a full and satisfying life. On top of that, she had recently solved a difficult case and been rewarded with quite a pile of money, and even though everyone knew the old saw about how money can't buy happiness, did anyone really believe it? And there was nothing but good news in every direction. Usually a dreary time of year for bookings, her *gîte* business was booked to overflowing for the following week thanks to a marketing campaign she had sent out playing up what a romantic place La Baraque would be for Valentine's Day. Benjamin Dufort, the handsome and complicated former chief of *gendarmes*, was back in town. And yet...

She stood at the window looking out, and moping.

Eventually Molly decided some company might help her out of her funk. So she bundled up, gave Bobo a pat, and hopped into her new Citroën coupe since it was too cold to use the scooter. The car had been a total splurge—and a silly one at that—since she didn't actually care all that much about what kind of car she drove. There was something about suddenly being rich that had made her lose her head for just a bit, and the car was the least of it.

La Baraque now had three new guest rooms in a formerly dilapidated wing off the main house where she lived. A swimming pool was being put in, with work beginning next month. Her bathroom had been renovated to a level of luxury that sailed right past "lap of" and landed a little over the top. Next month, a part-time gardener was due to start work.

While all these things were delicious in many ways—and to be honest, she didn't regret a single one of them—she nonetheless woke up every morning and, well, there she was. Same Molly, with the same ungovernable tangle of red hair, the same yearning for motherhood, the same uncertainty in the area of romance, and the same pants that were getting too tight.

She reminded herself on the ride into the village that it's not exactly charming to complain about how coming into a sudden windfall isn't as transformative as you thought it would be. After parking, she took a moment to look inside the big window of Chez Papa, the bistro that had become her second home in Castillac. She was friends—as everyone was—with the shaggy-headed owner, Alphonse, and knew she could count on knowing at least one person if she dropped by for a meal or a drink or a quick plate of *frites*.

That night, to her relief, her pal Lawrence sat on his usual stool, drinking his usual Negroni. He grinned when he saw her looking through the window.

"Trying to catch us up to no good?" he asked with a twinkle in his eye as she came inside.

Molly shrugged. "Oh, you know...I just like observing sometimes instead of jumping right in. So how are you? It's so strange to be at Chez Papa without Nico, isn't it?"

"I got a postcard yesterday, which pleased me inordinately. I didn't expect to get anything but the odd text."

Nico, the bartender, and his girlfriend Frances—Molly's best friend from home—had taken off for a month in the Maldives.

"Frances sent me a few photos. I'm *so* envious. That beach! That crystal-clear blue water!"

"I know. Well, why didn't you go with them? Something remains of your huge pile of gold, does it not?"

"Eh, who wants to be a third wheel? Plus, I have a big week coming up—I'm fully booked for Valentine's Day. Not that I'm not grateful. This time last year, I was about to start eating cat food, my income was so low."

"Well, my dear, no one is more pleased than I that your financial picture has become so rosy. Are you feeling the letdown yet?"

Molly jerked in Lawrence's direction. "Letdown?"

"Of course. Something big like coming into money, or winning a longed-for prize, finally accomplishing something you've worked for after years of effort, those sorts of things—I would imagine close to a hundred percent of the time—people get totally depressed afterwards. Ecstasy, followed by morosity. Because of course, getting the thing is wonderful, but it doesn't actually change you."

"Honestly, sometimes I think you live inside my brain."

Lawrence just smiled and sipped his drink. "I hope at least you've continued to spend the money frivolously?"

"I need to invite you over so you can take a gander at my bathroom."

Lawrence laughed. "Oh, I do love a bathroom makeover. Is it very trashy?"

"Lifestyles of the Rich and Not-at-All Famous *allll* the way."

They laughed.

"And, if I may be so nosy...what about Ben? Have you seen him lately?"

Molly shrugged again. "I don't know. It's...unsettled. I was so glad to see him when he got back, and I'm pretty sure he felt the same way. But now...we're being sort of careful around each other, you know? Friendly, interested...but a little..."

"Wary?

"Yes. If something's going to happen, someone needs to make the first move, but we're both waiting to see what the other one is going to do."

"What do you want to happen?"

"If I knew that...."

❧

CONSTANCE LEANED AGAINST THE DOORSILL, her arms crossed. "If you want my opinion, Molls—and of course I know you're dying for it, haha!—you should just get over yourself and get back together with Ben. You've been moping around ever since he got back. What are you waiting for?"

"Okay, yes, I admit there's been some moping. But I don't think that's why. Really, I don't."

"Then why do you get that pained expression on your face whenever I talk about how crazy-good things are going with Thomas now? I think it's because you feel left out. I'm blissfully in love, your buddy Frances is blissfully in love, and where are you? Staying home to eat almond croissants all night and day?"

"I'll have you know I've moved on from almond croissants. Haven't eaten one in weeks."

"Moved on to what, *pain au chocolat?*"

"I thought it was a nice change of pace."

"Molly!"

Molly heaved a theatrical sigh. "All right, I'll give him a call if it will stop your nagging. I do want things to work out between us, it's just that...I don't know, we're just taking our time. Which is why I don't think my grump has anything to do with him."

"Call him!"

"I said I would, jeez. Here's the mop, Mademoiselle Bossy."

Molly picked up a bucket and the vacuum cleaner. "Let's hit the cottage first," she said. They didn't bother putting on coats for the short walk over. The heat was only set at fifty degrees since no one was staying there, and they shivered as they came inside.

"Oops, sorry about the heat." Molly sat down on the sofa and stared into space.

Constance put down the window cleaner and a pile of rags and looked at her friend. "Molly?"

"Yeah?

"Is it okay if I turn up the heat?"

Molly looked at her vacantly as though she had lost the ability to understand French.

"Molls, are you feeling all right?"

Molly sighed again. "Actually, now that you mention it, no. I don't feel sick, exactly. But I'm so tired. Like I could sit here on this sofa pretty much into eternity and never get up."

Constance felt her forehead. "You don't have a fever."

"I don't feel sick. Just tired."

"It's probably your liver. You've got to go see Dr. Vernay. The village doctor—you've met him? He delivered most of us in Castillac. He's very good, he'll fix you right up."

Molly's expression didn't change.

"Want me to take care of it? I'll make the appointment and drive you over. In the meantime, why don't you just get in bed and rest? The guests aren't coming until tomorrow. I can do the cleaning in here by myself no problem."

"You're a doll."

"I know."

"I can't believe I've got six guests coming tomorrow. I've never had more than four at one time. What if they're all high maintenance?"

"It's Valentine's Day. They'll be busy with each *other*," said Constance with a wink.

"Oh please, let that be true," Molly muttered to herself, after thanking her friend and heading back to her house and bed. For once, she thought, let there be no drama. Just an easygoing crowd that gets along and needs no hand-holding.

She climbed into bed, and lacking the energy or commitment to protest when Bobo curled up next to her, fell fast asleep.

2

After a long nap followed by ten solid hours of sleep, Molly felt refreshed on Saturday morning and ready to face the influx of guests at La Baraque. She decided to skip the market—a first since moving to Castillac almost a year and a half ago—and instead made the rounds of all the guest rooms, making sure each was spotless and stocked with a welcome bottle of wine, along with a small booklet with suggestions for sight-seeing, restaurant recommendations, and some emergency phone numbers.

All in all, her gîte business was much more settled than it had been even six months earlier. The income was not substantial but it was steady-ish and improving. Molly now knew what to expect and felt ready for the odd questions guests sometimes came up with. And most important—she really liked doing it. The plumbing repairs, greeting guests and getting to know them, making improvements at La Baraque...there wasn't any part of the business that Molly minded, and most of it she thoroughly enjoyed.

Valentine's week was going to be a challenge, however. Fully booked, which at this point meant six guests: two couples and two singles. Darcy and Ira Bilson were due early Saturday morning; they had been traveling in the area and asked if they could check in early, which was fine with Molly since she had no guests currently in the cottage and the cleaning was long since done. By nine o'clock, Molly was up and caffeinated, expecting the Bilsons to show up any minute, and the rooms were all double-checked and ready.

Lately she'd been having a bowl of fruit in the morning instead of her usual croissants, not so much from any grand ambitions of self-improvement and control, but more for a change of pace. It had taken months to get over her habit of shoving food into her mouth while standing by the sink (or in front of the open refrigerator) instead learning to follow the French way, really taking time to make the meal an event even if she was eating by herself.

She sat at the table and sliced an apple into pleasingly thin and symmetrical slices. The orange cat streaked through the kitchen as though on a crucial mission from Satan, prompting Bobo to jump up in hot pursuit.

After polishing off the apple and her second cup of coffee, Molly got up to toss a few more logs into the woodstove. She heard a car pulling into the driveway. Slipping on a coat and grabbing a wool hat, she went quickly outside to greet the new guests.

"Bonjour, Madame Bilson!" she said, as a lean, dark-haired woman dressed in yoga pants got out of the small car. Her hair was cut short and her body so boyish that for a moment, Molly was confused, but she quickly got her bearings. "Monsieur Bilson! Welcome to La Baraque."

"Ah, we are thrilled to be here. Just thrilled! We're coming from three days at an organic farm north of here, not far from Limoges," said her husband as he came to shake Molly's hand. He was a big bear of a man, and stood with his chest expanded and hands on hips. His blond hair was shaggy and looked as though it hadn't seen a comb in a few days, and his eyes were red, perhaps from the strain of traveling.

"A working farm, with gîtes too?"

"Sort of, yes, they have a work program. So our room cost almost nothing, meals were free, and we put in some hours working on the farm every day. I milked a goat for the first time!"

Molly laughed. "You have to come back in the spring after the baby goats are born. There is nothing in this world cuter than a baby goat!"

"Affirmative, Molly!" boomed Ira. He was dressed in black jeans and a ripped black T-shirt, sort of a thirty-five-year-old's post-punk outfit. "This is a research trip for us. We're planning to start a cheesemaking business back home in Oregon, with our own goat herd. That's why we chose Castillac for this leg of our trip. Maybe you know Lela Vidal, who makes the incredible *Cabécou de Rocamadour*? She's quite famous in the cheese world."

"Yes, I do know her. Lela's at the Saturday market every week, and I've bought her excellent cheese many times. I had no idea she was a cheese celebrity."

Darcy shot Molly a dark look. "People who are good at their craft do develop reputations, you know. That is not in the least unusual."

Molly looked confused. "Sorry? I didn't mean...I wasn't being critical. Um, the Saturday market is going on right now. If you like, I'll show you the cottage, you can put your bags away and I'll take you to meet her."

"Excellent!" boomed Ira.

Molly was so used to the softer voices of her village she nearly clapped her hands over her ears, but caught herself in time. She picked up an extra bag that Ira Bilson had taken out of the car and walked toward the cottage. "We're still in late winter, obviously," she said. "Today's weather is very typical. Sometimes it seems as though we never see the sky in February! But the cottage is very dry and cozy, and you'll find a stack of firewood under the eaves to the right of the door."

"Is there an extra charge for that?" asked Darcy.

"Oh no," said Molly. "Everything's included, and I believe you're paid in full, so no worries on that score."

Darcy gave a brief nod but did not soften her expression. Although she was only thirty, a deep furrow had been carved between her eyebrows.

Tough nut, thought Molly.

"The bedroom is right through there, the bath is off to the left. Anything you need, just give a holler, I'm right in the main building. You can text me or just knock on the door. Would you like some time to settle in, or would you prefer to head straight to the market?"

"Let's go! Er...is that what you want to do, lovey?" he asked his wife.

Darcy shrugged.

"If you'd like to do yoga beforehand, that's fine too," he said. "Though I do want to have a crack at Lela's cheeses before they're all bought up."

Darcy sighed and shrugged again. "All right," she said, her tone one of deepest martyrdom.

Darcy jumped into the front seat of the Citroën leaving Ira to fold his long legs into the back. Molly turned the car around and pulled onto *rue des Chênes* and headed into the village. "Well, maybe I was silly to drive," she said, seeing that cars were parked far away from the village center, a sign that the market was crowded and parking places not easy to find. "I just got the car recently and I guess the excitement hasn't quite worn off. It's a perfectly pleasant walk, takes about fifteen minutes."

Ira opened his mouth to speak but closed it again. Darcy looked out of the window and said nothing.

Maybe more pain in the butt than tough nut, Molly thought. Not that I should judge anyone after five minutes...

She spotted a family getting into a Saab and waited patiently before easing into their spot. "All right!" she said brightly. "Would you like me to take you around and make some introductions, or set you loose? Either is fine with me, of course."

The Bilsons answered at the same time, with Ira wanting Molly's company and Darcy wanting to be without her. Darcy won, which did not come as a complete surprise to Molly. She pointed to the section of the market where the cheesemonger usually set up, and fled for the *Café de la Place*.

"Pascal!" she said, slipping into a seat on the glassed-in terrace where a small heater was set up. The model-handsome server grinned and asked her how she was doing.

"Fine, thanks. But I'll be even better if you'll bring me the Special." Pascal winked and disappeared into the kitchen. Molly was known in the village for her passion for French pastry, and croissants in particular. The café got theirs each morning from the best *pâtisserie* in the entire *département*—Molly's holy of holies, *Pâtisserie Bujold.* In less than a minute, Pascal was back with the Special on a tray: a large cup of steaming *café crème*, a tall and narrow glass of freshly squeezed orange juice, and a croissant on its own small plate. Molly sipped the coffee and thought about the Bilsons. One crabby spouse whom the other constantly tried to appease—was that a workable arrangement? Were they happy like that, or was Darcy on the verge of leaving because Ira never quite managed to mollify her? Or was Ira on the brink of storming off, having had enough of his impossible wife?

Molly's own marriage had ended years ago, but she reflected that she and Donnie had always seemed to get along, on the surface at least. They hadn't revealed anything like the public tension of the Bilsons. Yet what had that mattered? They had split up anyway, and Molly no longer regretted it, not now that the whole painful thing was far in the past.

The orange juice provided the perfect mixture of tart and sweet, and after drinking most of it, she turned her attention to the croissant. Leaving all ruminations on marriage behind, she bit into the slightly hard tip, the crunch so buttery and satisfying, and then another quick bite to reach the soft, stretchy inside that tasted vaguely of cheese (even though she knew there was no actual cheese involved). She couldn't help eating the whole thing more quickly than it deserved.

As she lingered over her coffee, reminding herself to pick up two other guests that afternoon at the train station, the Bilsons entered the café and sat down behind her. Molly started to speak but they did not appear to notice her, so she turned back around and edged her chair a bit closer, never one to pass up an opportunity to eavesdrop.

3

Not long after returning to La Baraque, two more Americans showed up: Ashley and Patty, two women from South Carolina who were celebrating Ashley's recent thirtieth birthday, and were staying in the renovated *pigeonnier*.

"I've been wishing to get to France practically my whole life," Ashley gushed, after giving Molly a warm hug. "My ancestors were French, you know. And the instant I set foot here, right in the Paris airport, I just felt...at home, in a way?"

"I completely understand," said Molly with a smile. Ashley was medium-height and curvy, with an impressive bosom and small waist that Scarlett O'Hara would have envied. She wore a pile of bangles on each arm, trendy ankle boots, and an eye-poppingly pink dress. Her blonde hair came from a cheap dye job, Molly noticed, not judging her for it.

Ashley's friend, Patty McMahon, did not hug. She smiled uncertainly when Molly welcomed her, looking embarrassed. She was very short, her pale skin scattered with freckles, brown hair in a long pixie cut. She dressed so plainly in jeans and a flannel shirt that Molly wondered what the two women had in common.

"So, how did you meet?" she asked.

"Back at Auburn? We were sorority sisters," said Ashley, putting her arm around Patty and squeezing her close. "Were you in a sorority, Molly?"

"Afraid not," Molly shook her head.

"Well, it's not all candles and lace, you know. When you're rushing, they put you through the most awful tests! I had to go to classes for an entire week wearing the ugliest pair of shoes known to mankind! Damn, I tear up just thinkin' about it."

Patty chuckled.

"Now Patty here?" Ashley continued. "She was a gift from God, I will tell you what. You've got to understand, if the girls catch you cheating on one of the tests, you're out, out out! And I...well, I was cheating. I just couldn't wear those hideous shoes everywhere I went. What would people think? And so one day I was walking to the sorority house wearing this pair of platforms that made my legs look like Elle McPherson's. I was planning to switch shoes when I got close, you see? But Lord Almighty, here comes a sorority sister (and not one of the nice ones either) and I thought, Damn it all to hell, my goose is cooked!

"But Miss Patty appears out of the blue, sees what's about to happen, and runs over to that sister with some story about a toaster being on fire, and I had time to slip into the ladies' room and put those ugly shoes back on. Had to leave the platforms behind though—you can't run around holding the evidence and not expect to get caught!"

"True enough!" said Molly, leading them to the pigeonnier and getting them settled just in time to go greet the next guest, Nathaniel Beech, dropped off in the driveway by Christophe, the taxi driver. Nathaniel looked lost, his gangly arms dangling at his sides, carrying his belongings in a high-tech backpack.

"Bonjour!" said Molly. "Are you Nathaniel or Ryan?"

"Nathaniel," he answered, looking a bit alarmed.

"Sorry, we're full up for this week and I'm expecting another single man to arrive any time. Welcome to La Baraque and let me show you to your room. Do you mind if I ask how you found out about the place?"

"Just web surfing. I've been wanting to visit France for a long time, and finally had enough vacation time saved up."

"Glad to hear you stumbled onto my website. My marketing efforts could be a little sharper."

"Oh, not at all. Your SEO wasn't bad at all, and hey, you're all booked up, so it's working pretty well, eh?"

"SEO?"

"Oh, sorry, didn't mean to get technical. Search Engine Optimization. It just means how findable you are online. Anyway, I'm happy to be here. If you need any help with all these guests, just give me a shout."

"That's very kind of you, Nathaniel, I may well be shouting!"

Nathaniel and the other single man, Ryan Tuck, were staying in the newly fixed-up wing off the main house. The rooms had en suite bathrooms, but no kitchens, and thanks to Molly's suddenly fat bank account, the beds, linens, and everything else were of very good quality.

Tuck arrived soon after. "Molly," he said warmly, giving her a quick hug. "I'm so glad to be here. Your place is incredible! Look at the color of that stone. How old is the house?"

"Depends on which part you're talking about," Molly laughed, pleased that he was taking an interest, and also pleased, if she were honest, to gaze on Ryan's chiseled features and buff body. He was wearing a rather tight T-shirt that showed off his muscles, and had dark brown hair cut short enough to stick straight up. Definitely an attractive guy, and with several single women at La Baraque, and Valentine's Day coming up, Molly thought there might be some interesting developments ahead.

After getting Ryan settled, Molly sneaked off to her bedroom for a breather. As much as she loved meeting new people, being responsible for the happiness of six guests all by herself felt a bit much at the moment. It was a dreary day with no sign of the sun, and her bedroom, far from the woodstove, was chilly. She pulled her new down comforter up to her chin, reached for her tablet, and dove into a new book.

After an hour of escaping to thirteenth-century England, she heard Bobo barking and got up to see what the dog was excited about. Glancing out a window in the hallway, Molly saw Ryan Tuck playing fetch. Bobo was dancing on her hind legs, waiting, and when Ryan threw the stick, she took off like a shot. Molly smiled. Of course, it was not at all the same as having a family, but still, it was very nice to have new acquaintances coming and going, and to see, in the short time they were there, they formed a sort of community. And she was, of course, always disposed to like anyone who made friends with Bobo.

It was 5:30 and time for a kir. She wandered into the living room, shoved another log in the stove to take the chill off, and reached for the bottle of crème de cassis.

A knock on the French doors.

"Hey Molly?" said Nathaniel through the glass.

"Oh hi, Nathaniel." She opened the door and let him in. "Is your room comfortable? You're the first to stay in that room since it's been renovated, so please let me know if there's anything amiss."

"It's very nice," answered Nathaniel, seating himself on a stool and watching Molly make her drink. "Hope I'm not bothering you? I'm a little at loose ends from arriving so late. Maybe you could tell me a good place to have dinner?"

"Oh, no bother at all! Would you like a drink? I'm making myself a kir, a very popular French drink that in my opinion is the most delicious cocktail in the world. But I have...let's see...I've got vodka, an open bottle of Bordeaux, Calvados that a guest left behind...."

Nathaniel tapped his chin. "I'll have what you're having," he said. "I wish my girlfriend could have joined me on this trip—she loves champagne more than anything. It's so much cheaper here, we could have had a bottle every night."

"Indeed," said Molly. "I'm sorry she couldn't make it. It's no good spending Valentine's Day away from your beloved."

Nathaniel nodded sadly. "I know. We haven't been together very long, and I'd booked the plane ticket ages ago. So she told me it would be crazy to waste it."

"Very understanding."

"Yes. Miranda's...well, she's a wonderful girl."

Nathaniel's cheeks got very red and Molly almost teased him but figured she didn't know him well enough. She put a kir in front of him and lifted her glass for a toast. "To Miranda!" she cried.

Banging on the front door. "Hold on, maybe someone else is thirsty," she said.

The Bilsons barged in as soon as Molly opened the door. "Bonsoir!" boomed Ira, laughing at his terrible accent.

"How was Lela Vidal?"

"Very friendly, very generous," said Ira. "We sort of invited ourselves over to her place tomorrow morning, right after the milking, so she can show us around. And in a stroke of luck, she's doing a workshop later on that we might want to stay over for."

"I've found people here to be really wonderful," said Molly, unsure how she felt about an extended Bilson stay.

"As long as you aren't killed," sniffed Darcy.

Molly paused, trying to master herself before she insulted one of her guests. "Are you talking about the very few murders that have occurred in the last few years?"

"Last few months, more like," said Darcy, with curled lip. "But no worries, Ira and I can take care of ourselves. I was wondering, can you recommend a place for dinner?" asked Darcy.

"Oh sure, Chez Papa is always open, if you're okay with bistro food. It's very good, just not fancy."

"Where is it?" asked Ira, rubbing his expansive belly. "I am *starving.*"

"If you go down rue des Chênes—the road we're on—and take the first fork to the left, it's a few blocks past that. A string of lights in the tree outside, the door is blue...I'd say tell 'em I sent you, but my bartender friend is on vacation and I don't know all the people filling in for him."

Ira was staring at Molly's refrigerator as though it were his only hope of survival.

"Or, I guess I could see what I've got here? I don't have enough food to cook for everyone, but I might be able to throw together a few hors d'oeuvres, if you're interested?"

Ira grinned broadly.

"Wonderful!" exclaimed Nathaniel, just as Ryan and Bobo came inside. "Now we don't have to go out into the cold, at least not yet."

Molly rummaged around in her cupboards and refrigerator; within ten minutes she'd put a tray of *gougères* in the oven, and placed a bowl of olives and one of marinated artichokes on the counter.

"I could live on hors d'oeuvres," she said, spooning more cheese puff dough onto a second tray. "Oh, I think I may have some prosciutto too—"

Ira made small talk with Nathaniel while Darcy stood with her arms crossed and a disagreeable expression on her face. Molly put all the alcohol she had on the counter along with some bottles of mineral water, and asked the guests to make themselves whatever they liked. "You know, I think this has officially turned into a party. I'm going to go let the other guests know they're welcome to join us. Ryan, will you take the gougères out in five minutes if I'm not back?"

Ryan grinned and saluted, and said he'd be glad to if she was willing to take the risk that he wouldn't run off with the entire tray for himself.

"I'll keep an eye on you," said Ira seriously, appearing to take Ryan's joke literally.

Grabbing her kir, Molly stepped out through the French doors and started down the path toward the pigeonnier. She breathed in deeply, enjoying the briskness of the cold air in her lungs, feeling a little happier now that her house was filled with people. Impulsively, she pulled out her cell and called Ben.

"Hello, Molly," he said, his voice soft.

"What are you up to? My gîtes are overflowing this weekend, and an impromptu party is starting up in my kitchen. Want to come over?"

Ben paused, just for a millisecond.

"I can't promise that the guests all get along," Molly continued. "But still, it's—" she was about to say "more fun than sitting home reading Napoleonic sea tales," but thought the better of it.

"On my way," said Ben, and Molly hung up, grinning like a schoolgirl.

MOLLY WENT AROUND to the pigeonnier to invite Ashley and Patty. Every time she looked at the building, she remembered Pierre Gault and admired the exquisite work he had done. There'll never be his equal when it comes to stonework, she thought.

She knocked lightly on the door. No answer, so she knocked again and called, "Ashley?"

"And you know I can't stand the smell of that soap. Really Patty, do you want me to have a migraine this whole entire time? Because that is what you have just set in motion. I can feel the pounding starting up already, it's like ocean waves gathering force, getting ready to crash on my poor little ol' head."

Ashley was talking so loudly that Molly did not have to rely on her eavesdropping superpowers to hear what she said. Was this going to be the Week of the Grouchy People? And I'm right there with them, she admitted to herself.

She rapped on their door. "Ashley? Patty?"

The door opened and Ashley greeted Molly with a wide grin, showing no sign of suffering from a headache. "Well, *bienvenue* darlin', come right on in! Patty and I were just thinkin' about having a little drink here in the room, and we'd be so honored if the *chatelaine* would join us! I took French in college, you know. Spent my junior year in Nice, and you know, going back in my family? We've got French people common as hen's teeth. Just love any and everything French, as I'm sure you understand!"

"Indeed I do," said Molly, thinking they had already had this conversation before. "Do you speak French too, Patty?"

Patty shrank back as though she wanted to be invisible, and Molly instinctively gave her more room.

"No," Patty whispered.

"I do all the talkin' around here!" laughed Ashley, fluffing up her hair.

"Well, I dropped by to tell you that the other guests are all downstairs in my living room. I'm making a few things for us to eat, and the party's just getting started! Please come down and join us if you'd like to. Completely casual of course, and whatever you want to do is fine."

"We were planning to have dinner in the village," said Patty.

"But Mouse, there's a *party* to go to! We don't want to miss that!"

Molly smiled. "All right! I've got things in the oven so I need to get back. *À tout à l'heure!*"

When she came back to the main house, she heard Darcy laughing uproariously, and Ira looking on as though he didn't get the joke.

"Ryan, you are just too funny!" Darcy said, her face now relaxed and open, her eyes even twinkling. Molly noted how a funny person would change the mood of a room in a blink of an eye, and she was grateful for Ryan's good humor. She bent down to peek in the oven, which was temperamental, sometimes disobeying the temperature controls and burning things to a crisp if she didn't keep an eye out.

"What are those delicious-looking morsels, anyway?" asked Ryan, standing at her elbow when she stood back up.

"Oh, gougères, one of my many French food obsessions. They're like cream puffs, only savory. Lots of grated gruyère to give them plenty of cheesy goodness."

Ryan laughed. "They sound amazing. And we're going to eat them hot out of the oven? Already, this vacation is turning out to be the best decision I ever made."

Molly eyed the young man. "Really? I hope you don't think this is unforgivably nosy, but I was wondering about you and Nathaniel, young men traveling by yourselves. What brings you to this backwater village where nothing much happens, in the dead of winter?"

"Ah," said Ryan with a quick smile. "Promise you won't make fun?"

"I can never promise that."

Ryan hooted. "Fair enough. Okay. My big secret is: I'm planning to start writing a novel. It's always been an ambition of mine, ever since I was a kid. I saved up so I could take a long time off work, and figured a change of scene—in a calm, peaceful sort of place—would be the way to help me get started. I'm hoping Castillac will boost my momentum so that when I head home, I can keep it going."

"Castillac looks a lot calmer than it is," murmured Molly, before brightening. "A novel! I love the idea of your starting a book here. I wish you the very best of luck."

"Thank you. No doubt, I can use every drop of luck you can send my way. You've already given me a good push in the right direction."

"How's that?"

"Well, I'm not really cut from the 'starving artist' mold, you know? I do enjoy my creature comforts." He flashed a smile that literally dazzled her, and she leaned her elbows on the counter and smiled back. "You've made La Baraque a real showplace. My room is the perfect combination of serenity and luxury. Call me shallow, but that's how I like to live. And I hope the atmosphere you've created will help me make a good start on my book."

Ryan put his hand on Molly's arm, and though she didn't wish it and wasn't looking for it, she felt a little spark of attraction. Their eyes met. "Please don't say anything to anyone about it," he said quietly. "It's just...you understand...not something I want just anyone to know. I'd rather not answer ten million questions about it. Kills the creativity, you know?"

"Of course, no problem. I am pretty good at keeping secrets," she said. "More or less."

Ryan looked at her with alarm.

"Sorry! Something about you makes me want to tease you." She laughed and took a sip of her kir and they looked at each other warmly and smiled.

"Darlings!" said a loud, Southern-accented voice, and everyone turned to see Ashley posing in the doorway with her arms open wide. "I want to know all of your names, starting with you!" She looked at Nathaniel and winked, and he stuttered out his name and moved away. Ashley spotted Molly in the kitchen and walked over with an exaggerated sway like she was on a Paris runway. "And who is this handsome specimen?" she said to Ryan, who introduced himself.

Ashley gave him a long look. "So," she said slowly, "you're the famous Ryan Tuck? The ladykiller known across all the southern states and probably up north too?"

"That sounds like a different Ryan Tuck," he laughed, and Ashley shrugged and sat down next to Ira, whispering in his ear. Patty looked down at the floor, and Molly went to her quickly and asked if she would like a drink. Before Patty could answer, Bobo barked and Molly excused herself to go to the door. "Ben!" she cried, and fell into his arms as though he had been away on another long trip.

"Well, *bonsoir* to you too," Ben deadpanned, hugging her tightly for an instant before letting her go. "I see you have a full house," he added.

"I know, you'd probably rather be home in bed reading. But I...I just wanted to see you. To be with you," she said, quietly so no one could overhear.

Ben slipped his arm around her and pulled her close. "Actually, there's something I'd like to talk to you about. Maybe this is a bad time?"

"No! Just let me get some hors d'oeuvres out and then we can take a little walk or something."

It did seem that the party was chugging along fine without any help from Molly. Ryan was whispering in Darcy's ear and she was giggling. Ira was nodding his head while Ashley lifted up the hem of her blouse a few inches and did what looked like a kind of belly dance in the middle of the room. Nathaniel was still sitting on the kitchen stool, drinking the same kir and looking amused. Patty was nowhere to be seen.

The gougères were perfectly golden brown, and Molly whisked the tray out of the oven and rolled them onto a wire rack to cool, biting into one and scorching the side of her tongue.

"I saw that," said Ryan, suddenly at her side.

Molly snickered. "Well, the cook has to make sure everything is all right before serving."

"Uh huh," he said, "sure. I'll be the official taste taster, if you don't mind." He picked up one of the puffs and put the whole thing in his mouth at once. "Oh oh oh," he said, and Molly wasn't sure whether he liked it or was burning his mouth to bits. "That was the most delicious thing I have ever eaten!" and impulsively he leaned forward, put one hand on her neck, and kissed Molly right on the mouth.

It was over so quickly she did not have to decide whether or not to kiss back.

"I'll pass them around?" said Ryan, quickly putting them on a plate and winking at Molly as he went out to the others.

Just then, with a rush of cold air, Patty returned, and stood awkwardly near the front door. Molly saw Ben looking at her, and she skittered her glance past him as though she had done something wrong, even though she was protesting in her mind that she had not. How had everything gotten so tangled up all of a sudden?

"Maybe I'll come back another time," he said, putting his coat back on.

"Oh, Ben," said Molly. "The guests—"

"I know. They want your attention, and you should give it to them." And before she could get another word out, the door was shut and he was gone.

4

Sunday mornings were usually very quiet in Castillac, especially if the night before had been as much fun as the party at La Baraque had been. Molly knew it was nothing but luck, but for some reason, the guests who had been so grouchy on their own had been brilliant once they were all together, getting along like gangbusters and staying up talking and drinking until long after midnight.

Bobo woke Molly up by licking in her ear. "Bobo! Quit that!" she said, reluctantly sitting up and rubbing her eyes. She had not had too much to drink, she was thankful of that. She guessed she might be the only one waking up at La Baraque that morning without a terrible hangover. While she waited for the coffee to finish dripping, she texted Ben asking if he would like to meet her at the café de la Place for breakfast. No answer right off, which probably meant he was out for a run. She hoped so, anyway, feeling both curious about what he had wanted to talk to her about, and a little worried that he had seen Ryan flirting and gotten the wrong idea.

And it *was* the wrong idea. It was a little unsettling, at nearly forty, to find herself still vulnerable to sudden attractions and charming men—but it was all harmless enough.

Wasn't it?

It wasn't as though she were actually interested in Ryan, though he was pretty adorable. But did it...did it mean anything that sparks could still fly with other men? Did it mean Ben was not really The One?

There's no such thing as The One, she could hear Frances telling her, and she was probably right. Not that twice-divorced Frances was an expert on relationships...though Molly supposed one could argue she did have more experience than most people. She glugged down a cup of coffee and decided to go for a walk. She would head into the village, in case Ben wanted to meet, and if not, she could use the exercise and fresh air to clear her mind.

It was cloudy again, and chilly, but not really cold. By now Molly was an expert at French methods of scarf-tying, and her pretty, green mohair scarf set off her red hair nicely and kept her throat warm, all while looking quite chic by the standards of Castillac. No cars on rue des Chênes, only a crow cawing in an oak. She passed the cemetery with *Priez pour vos Morts* written in the ironwork over the gate, and thought for a moment about those buried there. Pausing at the gate, she considered going in and paying her respects, but a growl from her stomach convinced her to move along toward civilization and croissants.

The air was damp and she took deep breaths, still not feeling quite right, as though the effort to move was twice as exhausting as it normally was. Just as she reached the Place—almost deserted on a Sunday morning—she felt her cell vibrate in her pocket and drew it out. A text from Ben:

On my way

She felt relieved and quickly headed for the Café de la Place, looking forward to its warmth, the friendly face of Pascal, and of course, the Special. Before Pascal had a chance to come over, Ben slid into the seat across from her and looked at her coolly.

"Late night?" he asked, looking down at his phone as though he were receiving a number of important messages that very minute.

"Yes, it was. It was the strangest thing. Almost everyone was in really bad moods when I first met them yesterday—complaining, hard to please, grouchy. I was thinking, oh man, it's going to be a long week. But then they ended up in my kitchen, and like magic, once they were all together, you'd think they were best pals. Laughing and telling their life stories, happy as clams."

"And the fellow in the kitchen with you, was he in a bad mood yesterday too?"

Molly considered. "No, not really. I think he might be the person who...Ryan's very good humored...." She looked at Ben and saw that he was grim-faced. "Now Ben, don't be...are you mad at me? Really?"

He narrowed his eyes for a second longer and then forced himself to smile. "Of course not," he said, signaling to Pascal. "It's not like we...I mean, we're free to...don't have any..."

Molly laughed. "We're not official."

He gave a quick nod, then his expression softened and he reached for her hand. "I missed you when I was away."

Molly smiled and squeezed his hand, and she felt a strange and wonderful sensation of happiness spreading through her body as they looked at each other. "I missed you too," she whispered.

"Then maybe you'll be interested in something I'd like to propose," Ben said, waving again for Pascal, who was talking animatedly to a couple of young women seated on the other side of the room.

Molly's knees went weak at the word *propose*. She was stunned.

"Of course I did a great deal of thinking on my trip to Thailand," Ben said. "That was the point of the trip, obviously. Back when I was working on Rémy's farm, he kept talking to me about my mission in life."

"I'm guessing he didn't think it was farming?"

Ben laughed. "Correct. He is convinced that everyone has a mission. Doesn't have to be anything terribly ambitious—he means something you are very well suited for, something that will...well, he gets a little spiritual about it and I don't quite follow him that far, but at any rate...my mission, that's one of the main things I was thinking about as I rode elephants and surfed and ate curry."

At that point Molly's face had taken on a frozen aspect, as she tried and failed to master her emotions. Hadn't he said *propose?* What did that have to do with Rémy and curry?

"My decision to quit the *gendarmerie*, as you know, was not made hastily. I don't regret it. And you remember—"

Molly missed the next few sentences as she took in the knowledge that whatever Ben had to say, it was not going to involve marriage. She was surprised by how disappointed she felt.

"—when we met, there were three cases, three girls: Amy Bennett, Valerie Boutillier, and Elizabeth Martin. Two down, one to go. I found myself lying on the beach and going over the facts in the Martin case, trying to think of a new way to approach it. I can't let it go, Molly. And—it's not just the Martin case, it's doing that kind of work that I can't let go. Bringing violent people to justice, giving friends and families of the victims the comfort that at least justice was served. It sounds silly that it took going to Thailand to allow me to understand that about myself—and I didn't say anything about it when I first got back because I wondered if it was a sort of fever dream of the tropics, and once I was back in Castillac, I would lose heart all over again."

Molly nodded, trying to look sympathetic, her face awkwardly frozen.

"This is terribly long-winded of me, very sorry. Is Pascal ever going to get to us?" He turned and waved at the server, who waved back but did not leave the table with two young women.

"You said you had something to ask me?" Molly said, her voice catching, to her horror.

"Yes! I'm getting to that. All right, so...I still want to do detective work, definitely. I believe I have worked out the reasons for my anxiety, and actually, I want to continue whether that remains a problem or not. But the gendarmerie is a closed door now, and besides, I would have been transferred very soon anyway, and my heart belongs to Castillac. I want to do the work here. And so my question for you, Molly: would you like to be my partner? Would you like to make a business with me, as private investigators?"

When Ben said the word 'partner', her heart skipped another beat. I am being *ridiculous*, she told herself, taking a deep breath and letting what he was saying sink in. "Well, that sounds incredible, actually. But would there be enough work in a village this small?"

"No. Nowhere close. We would have to do a bit of traveling—certainly to Bergerac and Périgueux, and if we develop a good reputation, we might get work anywhere in France, or perhaps Europe. Depends on what sort of career you want, and how successful our cases are. But we work very well together, Molly Sutton. The fact that we don't always agree is, in my opinion, a positive thing." He cocked his head and waited for her answer. "So? What do you think?"

She didn't know whether to pop him one on the head or quickly agree. It was a wonderful and tempting offer, for sure. But how could such a kind and lovable man be so infuriating?

THE WALK back from the village was tiring, despite fortification from the Special, and Molly wished she had driven. I must be getting old, she thought, unused to feeling fatigue from such moderate exertion. As she approached the driveway to La Baraque, she saw Nathaniel Beech walking toward her from the other direction.

"Bonjour, Nathaniel," she said as they got close. "Out for a morning walk?"

"I'm afraid I got a little turned around," he said sheepishly. "I was headed into Castillac for some breakfast but I guess I went the wrong way."

"I picked up some croissants while I was there, would that do?"

"Thanks! Can't go wrong with a fresh croissant."

"A man after my own heart. So, did you have a good time last night? Sometimes my guests keep to themselves, which is totally fine, but it was nice to see everyone jump in and make friends like that."

"I did enjoy myself, thanks. I'm just...it's all a little...this is my first trip out of the country. So everything's a bit overwhelming."

"It's not easy traveling alone if you're not used to it. Especially if you don't speak the language."

"I studied Spanish in school, unfortunately."

"Not unfortunate at all! I'm dying to go to Madrid. And Sevilla is supposed to be incredible! You can plan a trip with Miranda."

Nathaniel beamed. "You're very kind to remember. It must be something to have all these guests streaming through, telling you their life stories."

Molly laughed. "Oh, it's interesting, believe me! I've had some real characters." She thought fleetingly of the odd Wesley Addison, who was coming back in June for two weeks. Nathaniel followed Molly into the kitchen. She put the croissants on a platter and went to make more coffee. Darcy Bilson showed up at the French doors with bedhead, announcing that their coffeemaker had blown up, and could she beg for some. Then

Patty knocked timidly at the front door, wanting to know if Molly had any aspirin for Ashley's headache, though only a few minutes later, Molly saw Ashley and Ryan huddled in a corner looking like they were solving the problems of the world together.

And in the space of twenty minutes, Molly's kitchen had filled with all six guests, greeting each other like long-lost family members. They drank pots of coffee and ran through the bag of croissants in minutes, comparing hangovers and laughing at in-jokes from the night before. Ashley reprised her belly dance without any music, Nathaniel sat on his stool chuckling, Ryan was again at Molly's elbow looking for ways to help as she served up the sausage she had bought for her own dinner that night, along with a platter of scrambled eggs with a good grating of Cantal over the top. Ira Bilson's booming voice punctuated the swirl of chatter. Darcy was doing a headstand in a corner of the room.

With all the socializing and hostess duties, she almost forgot about Ben and his "proposal," but in the back of her mind, she felt a kind of tingle, because as much as she loved running La Baraque—and she couldn't imagine giving it up—the idea of being a real live private investigator was thrilling. The fact that a real live former police detective thought she'd make a good one only heightened the charge. She had read every single Nancy Drew mystery when she was young, and identified thoroughly with the titian-haired detective. The times she had been able to help out with cases in Castillac had been the most satisfying of her life.

Maybe better than marriage, she mused, smiling to herself as she chopped some parsley to sprinkle over the eggs.

"You don't want to get on her bad side, I can tell you that much," Patty was saying to Ira. Molly pricked up her ears.

"Oh come on, she looks sweet as pie," said Ira.

"That's just the Southern accent. Do not be fooled," answered Patty in a low voice. "I've known her since we were in the same sorority back at Auburn. Yeah, okay, don't look so surprised. I got sympathy votes because my mother died during Rush Week, otherwise I'd never have gotten in and Ashley and I wouldn't be friends. But what I was going to say..." she leaned in close to Ira's ear and Molly leaned too but missed some of what Patty was saying. "...police were called...had to wear a wig after that..." was all she got.

Ashley was sitting on a stool next to Nathaniel. "Well, aren't you just the cutest thing," she said, batting her eyelashes at him in what had to be an ironic fashion. "Let me guess—you are a technology wizard, isn't that right? Know every little last thing about computers?"

Nathaniel blushed all the way to his hairline. "Well, I wouldn't say that. You can never know everything about anything."

Ashley tapped a fingernail on his forearm. "But I'm right, aren't I, about computers? What lucky place has you working for them?"

"I work in IT, at a hospital. Lot of data goes through a hospital of course, and you'd be surprised at how backward most of their systems are. It's even been a struggle getting some of the doctors on board with basic email."

"Well, I never heard of such a thing," said Ashley distractedly. She was watching Ryan put his arm around Molly's shoulders and say something in her ear that made her laugh.

"You are such a bad influence," Molly said to him, grinning.

"I'm sure you have a little champagne squirreled away somewhere, I can tell just by looking at you. You're a woman who likes to celebrate, and in France that means champagne! Or is that just a cliché?"

"No, no, the French in fact do love their champagne. Who wouldn't?"

"You *do* have some."

"Yes."

"Well, come on! I'll buy it from you, it'll be my treat for everyone. Look at how much fun your guests are having! And they'll have even more fun if you spike their orange juice with a splash of champagne."

"It's a waste, drinking it that way."

"Well, I'm not picky, where are your flutes? I'll get them out and set everything up." He smiled at her then, such a winning smile of warmth and good humor, of wanting to give others pleasure while getting plenty for himself, that she couldn't say no.

Not that she wanted to anyway. He was standing close to her and she put her hands on his broad chest and pushed him back a few inches. "Oh, all right, champagne it is. It's practically lunch time now anyway. But I have to warn you, it's not cold..."

"It's an eagle," Ira was saying to Patty. He pushed the sleeve of his T-shirt higher so that she could see the entire tattoo.

"Are you some kind of rah-rah nationalist or something?" she asked, her nose wrinkling.

"Are you some crazy liberal or something?" he shot back, pulling his sleeve down. Darcy appeared at his side, taking his chin in her hand and turning his face toward her for a kiss. "We are not going to be talking politics on this vacation," she said matter-of-factly.

Ryan came over with a tray and several flutes of champagne. "Take one, everybody! Seize the day!"

"I've used up my alcohol allotment for the week in the first twenty-four hours," mumbled Ira.

"Oh come on, now," said Darcy, stroking his bicep. "A little splurge would be good for you." They each took a glass, Ira managing a slight smile as Darcy rubbed his back.

"Three cheers for Molly!" Ryan shouted to the crowd, and they all lifted their coffee mugs or champagne flutes and cried out "Three cheers for Molly!" while Molly opened the narrow closet where she kept wine and brought out two more bottles.

It seemed like such a convivial, happy moment—the group of strangers all crowded into Molly's kitchen, laughing and getting to know each other, wanting their vacation to be as special as possible. They thought—or at least most of them did—they were making real friends, people they would keep up with once they returned home. But instead of reminiscing about the carefree time they'd spent in Castillac, those phone calls of the future would turn out to be something quite different indeed.

5

When Molly woke the next morning, she wriggled back under the warm covers and thought about Ben's private investigator idea. After the Amy Bennett case, she had briefly considered hanging out a detective shingle herself. But as kind and welcoming as the *Castillaçois* had been since she moved there, she thought that perhaps hiring an expat with no actual training in investigative work might be a stretch. And it could look as though she were trying to capitalize on the unfortunate events that had been occurring far too often around Castillac lately. But with Ben Dufort as her partner? None of that would matter at all. Being in business with Ben, who had grown up in Castillac and knew absolutely everyone, would give her all the credibility anyone could ask for.

She was thrilled he thought highly enough of her detective abilities to ask her. All in all, once she got over the mild disappointment of the proposal being something other than what she had expected, Molly was excited about the idea and eager to talk over the details with him. She swung out of bed, wondering where Bobo had gotten to, and hoping to have at least one cup of coffee before any guests showed up.

But coming into the kitchen in her bathrobe, Molly saw Patty's face peering in through the French doors, and resignedly, she opened the door.

"Bonjour, Patty," she said weakly, "do you need something?"

Tiny Patty slipped inside, hopped on a stool, and put her elbows on the kitchen counter, looking for all the world like a fourth-grader waiting to be fed breakfast before the school bus arrived. Well, at least it was the quiet one, Molly thought.

"Hey. I was wondering if you have any tape? I'm planning to buy some souvenirs today and then send them home."

Molly looked confused. "You want tape to wrap a package, but you haven't bought the stuff that goes in the package yet?"

Patty nodded brightly. "Just getting organized."

"Um, there's scotch tape in the drawer in the living room. Packing tape...I don't think I have any of that. You can probably get it at the *Presse*, it's right on the Place, let's see...southwest corner. With all the newspapers out front."

"Did you see how angry Ira got yesterday?" Patty said, confidentially. Molly had the clear impression that she wanted to gossip more than find tape.

"Angry?"

"Oh, yes. After a few rounds of champagne, Darcy was in the corner talking to Ryan. I guess they got a little too close and Ira was absolutely *furious.* And you don't want a big guy like that mad at you, is all I'm saying." Patty delivered this news with relish.

Molly shrugged. "Well, as long as nobody started throwing punches, I guess we're okay." She stared at the coffee press, willing the brew to drip through faster.

"It's just sort of funny how people go on vacation, something they've probably saved up for and looked forward to for a long time, but they can't manage to leave all their resentments and jealousies behind. All of it gets packed in the suitcases along with the toothpaste and good walking shoes."

"You have a point," said Molly. "What's that saying? We take ourselves wherever we go."

"The seduction of travel," Patty said, leaning in so close that Molly backed away and pretended to look for something in the refrigerator, "is just the opposite, wouldn't you agree? That you can go somewhere foreign and be an entirely different person? Leave your boring old self and all your troubles behind, and be someone, I don't know, glamorous? Even dangerous?"

Molly laughed lightly. "I know what you mean. Though maybe not everyone is so unhappy with their regular lives. Or has such an imagination."

Patty hopped off the stool and came up close to Molly. She was so short that even Molly felt like a giant around her. Patty peered up through round glasses that were too big for her small features, nodding and gathering steam.

"You're welcome to have some coffee," said Molly, hastily pouring herself a cup and moving toward the door. "And any number of places in the village are open now if you'd like something to eat. Have a wonderful day exploring, and I'll see you later! Give my best to Ashley...."

Whew, Molly thought, closing her bedroom door. I just want to climb back into bed and pull the covers over my head.

Bobo came skidding over and licked her hand. "All right. Let's go for a walk. Just a short one, I really am tired. But maybe some fresh air will perk me up." She got dressed and left quickly before any other guests could appear.

Once in the woods, she felt immensely better. It was a cold morning and a dusting of frost still showed in spots where the sun hadn't hit. She walked across the meadow, footsteps crunching on frozen grass. Bobo sprang here and there, following her nose. Molly re-tied her scarf so that it covered her ears, and they entered the forest that backed up to Molly's property.

It was Molly's second February in Castillac and she felt as though she was just getting to know the woods in different seasons. She found the trail and walked slowly along, thinking about Ben and pondering what sort of business card she would get, now that she was about to become Molly Sutton, P.I.

She was thinking so hard about the design of the card that at first she didn't notice anything amiss. The forest was quiet, as though she and Bobo were deep in the wilderness, though La Baraque was just the other side of a copse of junipers. But then something caught the corner of her eye. Something was out of place, and she turned her head to see what it was.

Then she screamed. And once she really saw what it was, she put her hand over her mouth and said, "Oh, no. Oh, not *you.*"

6

Molly stood well back, watching as the forensics team did their work under the direction of Gilles Maron, acting chief of gendarmes in Castillac. The coroner, Florian Nagrand, stood with his hands folded on his big belly, looking around at the forest as though hoping to spot an interesting bird.

Molly walked over to him and asked, "Can't you cut him down?" She had never seen a hanged person before in real life, and it was far more horrible than she had imagined. She tried to keep her eyes down but she couldn't help it, she kept looking up at Ryan, dangling there, his limbs limp and his eyes unseeing.

"Soon, my dear," he said, still looking up into the trees. "You know, I once saw a gray-headed woodpecker in a tree like that. Quite rare, you know. Far too early in the year now, though."

"All right then," said Maron, walking over to Molly as Nagrand drifted away, still looking up. "I've got a few questions, if you don't mind, but it should be quick enough—there's nothing suspicious about this situation, we can say that, at least."

"Oh, there certainly is, Gilles. I know he's only been here for a few days, but I...I feel like I knew him...at least, I knew him well enough to say that it is impossible—okay, *highly* unlikely—that

Ryan Tuck killed himself. He was so energetic—sort of impish, really—the life of the party!"

Maron shrugged. "Eh, sometimes people hide their sadness very well. Perhaps being the life of the party was an attempt to distract himself, and ultimately, it failed. Well, *obviously* it failed."

"But if it's so clear what happened, why do you have forensics here?"

"I don't believe in leaving things to chance, Molly. Unless the body is of a ninety-nine year old with a heart condition, I'm calling forensics. And maybe even then," he added, with a rare attempt at a joke.

"But—"

Maron's deputy, Paul-Henri Monsour, approached. "Excuse me, Chief. Monsieur Nagrand would like to examine the body. We can get it down now?"

"As long as the team is done on the ground."

Monsour nodded and went to take care of it. Molly watched over Maron's shoulder as a young man climbed the tree as easily as though it were a ladder, and hacked at the rope with a sort of machete.

"This is beyond horrible," she murmured.

"Agreed," said Maron. "He's young and good-looking. A waste. Allow me to ask—is the tree in question within your property boundary?"

Molly looked confused. "Um...I don't think so, but I'd have to walk back and get out the map to make sure. My property does extend into the forest but not this far, I don't think. This section probably belongs to Madame Sabourin. What difference does it make?"

"Merely being thorough, as I'm sure you'll appreciate."

Molly suppressed a sigh. "I should get back home. The other guests are going to be in for a shock."

"Indeed. Had there been much interaction among the guests? How many do you have currently?"

"Six—now five. And yes, they are a social group. Extremely so."

"And how did Tuck seem, overall? You said 'life of the party'... so he was happy, convivial?"

"Absolutely. He told stories, made people laugh—he was the spark, you know?" Thinking of how he had cajoled the champagne out of her the day before made her eyes get moist. "He liked to celebrate," she added quietly.

"Well, I guess we all have sides that we don't show to others," Maron said.

Molly shook her head. "I'll never believe it. Even if it ends up proven that he struggled mightily with depression, I'll never believe he committed suicide. It's just not possible."

"You can't turn every death into a murder case, Molly."

Molly stared. "That's a low blow."

Maron shrugged again. "It wasn't meant as a blow, simply a statement of fact. Sometimes people's moods are unpredictable and they act impulsively. I'm afraid that was the case for Mr. Tuck. If you want to look on the bright side, if there is such a thing, at least he had a bit of fun in his last days, if it was not all an act."

Molly bit her lips to keep from speaking and walked away from Maron. Ryan was lying on the ground and the rope had been cut away. "Bless you," she said to him, feeling the inadequacy of the words but not able to come up with anything else.

"Ah, Molly," said Nagrand. "Always in the middle of everything, aren't you?"

"Put a sock in it," said Molly, and headed for La Baraque.

As Molly walked back to La Baraque, half-numb, she kept picturing the merry expression on Ryan's face the day before as he made the rounds, serving champagne to everyone. She thought of the way he would come into a room and immediately, everyone's spirits would lift. She thought of how he had charmed the grumpy Darcy, how he loved to be teased, how he had adored gougères with an intensity that made her feel they were food soulmates.

How he had kissed her.

He hadn't meant anything by it, she knew that. Nor had she wanted him to. It was only an example of the kind of irrepressible affection that made Ryan so popular with everyone.

She shook her head to push away the image of him dangling by his neck in the woods. It made no sense. Intellectually, she knew he was dead, of course. But it felt as though her whole body was revolting, working strenuously to reject the idea, to come up with some other explanation for the grisly event she had discovered: a terrible joke, a misguided prank, *something*.

Back inside by the woodstove, she let out a mournful sigh and squatted down to put her head on Bobo's speckled neck.

"Oh, Bobo, how in the world? How in the world can this have happened?"

She saw a flash in the corner of her eye, and turned to see Patty, once again standing by the French doors. Did these guests not ever plan to go sight-seeing? Patty waved and let herself in.

"Hi Patty, come on in." Molly wondered what the best way to tell everyone the news was. Well, there was no right way; nothing she did was going to soften the horror for all of them. "I'm afraid...I have some bad news."

"Uh oh," Patty said, but grinned as though she were starving and a terrific-smelling grilled steak had just appeared in front of her.

Molly sighed again, feeling as though she wasn't quite getting enough air. "It's Ryan," she began, and then she felt the force of tears beginning to come and she stopped talking to hold them back. Crying was all fine and well, but she would much rather do it in private.

Patty went on tip toes. "Yes?" she prodded. "Ryan?"

"It's unbelievable, but I'm afraid he's hanged himself. I found him a few hours ago, in the woods."

Patty stared. She blinked. "Hanged?"

"I'm afraid so."

Patty shook her head rapidly. "That's not...Ashley's not going to...."

"I know, it's going to be terrible news for everyone. Ryan was really the spark here these last few days, wasn't he?"

"I didn't have much to do with him."

Molly looked hard at the other woman. Because of her looks, it was sometimes hard to remember that she wasn't just a kid. Patty was a thirty-year-old in a child's body. And like some children, she seemed to focus on other people's bad behavior;, at least that was how she struck Molly in the moment.

"Did you get the idea Ryan was unhappy?" Molly asked.

Patty shrugged. "For sure I got the idea he wanted to *look* happy."

"Maybe. Though I have to say, if that's as deep as it went, he sure fooled me."

"So, now what? Do you want me to get everyone together so you can make an announcement?"

Molly considered for a long moment. "Okay, let's do it that way," she said finally. "I don't think I have it in me to break the news to everyone individually. Just repeating the words that many times would be more than I could handle."

Patty took off down the hallway on the way to her room. Molly put another log in the stove and looked out the window. If Ryan had been that sad, that desperate, how could I have missed it? Am I that callous? Were we all more interested in having a superficial good time than in really getting to know each other?

In a few minutes, Ashley wandered in, her blonde hair falling in curls past her shoulders, wearing white cowboy boots and a short skirt with fringe.

Molly smiled. "Love your outfit. It makes me smile, which at the moment counts for a lot."

Ashley looked confused. "Thank you. I do love some fringe. What's going on? Patty said you've got something to tell everybody? I hope it won't take too long because we're planning to drive over to Beynac to see the château, and there's this place I've read about where we're going to have a late lunch that is supposed to be absolutely divine—"

"An announcement?" boomed Ira, coming through the front door without knocking. "Did we win a prize? Is there food?"

Nathaniel knocked at the front door and came in, wearing a small backpack. Patty entered last and closed the door, her face expectant and a little excited.

"Thanks for coming over, everyone. I'm glad you were all still at La Baraque and hadn't set out on the day's adventures." She paused again, fighting back tears. "I wish there were some easy way to say this, but there absolutely isn't, so I'm going to just come out with it. I found Ryan in the woods this morning. He had hanged himself."

A long, silent pause.

"What did you say?" asked Darcy.

"Ryan is dead?" asked Ira.

"What?" said Nathaniel.

Ashley said, "No." Patty put her arm around her waist and hugged her from the side. "No!"

"I know it's really shocking," said Molly. "I can't imagine going on a long-awaited vacation, making friends, and then deciding to...to end it all before I even got home."

And it was at that moment that Molly decided that without more proof, she was not going to believe that Ryan Tuck had killed himself. If she had learned anything at all about detective work, it was that things are often not what they seem. You see a man hanging by his neck at the end of a rope tied to a tree, you assume he was the agent of his own death.

Well, maybe not.

She was able to hold her grief in check enough to spend the next minutes observing and then comforting her guests. Ashley was sobbing, crumpled on the floor, with Patty squatting beside her, making comforting noises. Darcy's back was to Molly; she stood at the window, immobile. Ira faced the group, his expression stoic, running a hand through his messy blond hair. Nathaniel stood staring at Molly, his eyes filling with tears.

"All right then," Ira said. "Are we done? Anything else?" The gruffness of his tone made everyone look over at him, startled.

"Ira!" said Darcy.

"What? You've known the guy for like two days, people. He wasn't your best friend. Stuff happens. Come on, Darcy, we've got an appointment with the cheesemonger over near Lalinde, and I don't want to be late."

"Get control of yourself, Ira," Darcy said quietly.

"Jerk," said Ashley.

"Well, I just hope this doesn't make everything weird from now on," said Nathaniel. "I mean, I'm traveling alone, and it's been really great meeting you guys and hanging out. It's made my vacation so much more fun than it would've been, what with my girlfriend stuck back at home and all."

Patty nodded. "I've really been having fun too. Thank you for being such a good hostess, Molly," she said, coming over and giving her a side-hug. "I'm thinking we should have some kind of, I don't know, service of some sort. Does anyone know if Ryan was religious?"

"He was not," said Ashley, still on the floor. "He believed in living for the moment, and that's it. At least that's what he told me yesterday when we were all having champagne. 'Forget about the past,' he told me. 'Live for right now!'" She put her hands over her face and let out a muffled sob. Nathaniel shook his head slowly, looking at the floor.

Molly took a deep breath. "All I can say is that...I'm just so sorry this has happened. This was supposed to be a week of exploration and fun, good food and happy times. And it really did start out that way, almost magically so. I hope we can all remember Ryan's spirit and how much he contributed to that magic. And also that you can all carry on and enjoy the rest of your vacation."

"Fat chance," said Darcy.

"How about we get in the car and scour the Dordogne for out-of-the way farms? We might discover a cheese hardly anyone knows about," said Ira, who had quickly regained some of his usual cheerfulness.

"Not everything is about food, Ira," said Darcy.

Molly stood listening, wanting to leave, to be by herself for five minutes, but her legs felt heavy and she couldn't find the momentum to move. She had chosen Castillac because she thought it was going to be peaceful and calm, and now there was another death, literally in her backyard. And as upsetting as the idea of suicide was, she had a feeling that the whole story—whatever it was—would be even more so. Not that she had any way of finding out what it was.

7

Bobo barked and Molly went to answer the door.

"I would like to have a look at Ryan's room," said Maron, as though he and Molly were already in the middle of a conversation. "I won't be long."

"Right, I was expecting you. I have an email address for him, that's all. What happens in a case like this, anyway? How do you contact the family?"

"There's never been a foreign death while I've been on the force," Maron admitted. "But my guess is that the embassy will handle it. I'd like to be able to give them his passport number to make the whole thing easier."

Molly nodded and led him down the hallway and into the wing where Ryan's room was. The house had been added to over the years in a haphazard manner, with some additions more solid than others. They zigzagged through a narrow passageway, an open room with new sofas and a coffee table, and then up a rickety set of wooden stairs.

She tried the door and found it unlocked. "Here you are," she said, pushing it open.

Maron strode in and looked around, hands on hips. The room

was neat. The bed was made, the small desk only had a scattering of coins on it, and a paperback from Molly's library was on the bedside table. There was no note.

For a moment Molly thought she smelled something, but when she sniffed, the scent seemed to evaporate.

"Where are his things?" asked Maron, baffled.

Molly went to the antique armoire that she'd bought at the flea market in Paris and had sent down. A small key was in the lock and she turned it, opening the door to reveal a zipped duffel, along with a few shirts and a sport coat on hangers. Maron lifted the duffel out and began to go through it.

"Did he have anything on him?" asked Molly. "Wallet or anything?"

"He did not. I'm hoping everything will be here."

And it was. In a side pocket of the duffel, Maron found Ryan's wallet, passport, and a set of keys.

"He sure was neat and organized," said Molly. "Do you think he wanted to make things easy after he was gone? Like he was being thoughtful about the people who would need to deal with the situation?"

"That would be extraordinarily caring from a person so severely depressed."

Molly shrugged. "Wouldn't put it past him. As I've said, never once did I get the impression he was depressed even a little."

"He was only here a few days, correct? And you weren't with him every minute? People, even depressed people, can hide their feelings. Especially for short periods, and from people who don't even know them."

"I guess," said Molly. The sight of Ryan's room, so devoid of his spirit and good humor, was bringing her even farther down than she already was. "Are you done? I think I'd better get back to my guests. They've obviously had quite a shock."

"I've got what I need," said Maron, briskly. Now that he had Ryan's passport, the case was soon going to be off his desk. He began to think of some tasks he could assign Paul-Henri Monsour that would keep him out of the station for the rest of the day so he could catch up on paperwork and enjoy some time alone.

Molly walked him to the front door and watched as the gendarme started up his scooter and took off down rue des Chênes. Normally very happy to be around people, she found herself wanting nothing more than to retreat to her bedroom. The idea of watching movies while under a pile of covers seemed like a holiday in heaven. Add some Côte d'Or chocolate bars (the kind with nuts and raisins) and the prospect was irresistible.

"Molly?" called Patty.

Taking a deep breath, she forced herself to return to the living room.

"We were thinking of some ideas for that memorial service...."

"You only knew the guy for a matter of hours," said Ira to Patty. "Can't we just move on with our vacation? I know I've got a long list of places I'd like to visit in the short week we'll be here."

"You're so unfeeling," Ashley said in a low voice.

Ira shook his head. "No, no I'm not. And in the very short time we knew him, we can definitely say Ryan would be the first person to tell us to seize the day, enjoy ourselves, and not mope around over things that can't be changed."

"He's got a point," said Nathaniel. "Maybe anyone who wants to could meet up to say a few words, remembrances or whatever, like tonight when everyone's back at La Baraque? I think I'm going over to Rocamadour today, if anyone wants to join me. Ashley and Patty, want to see an amazing church hanging off the side of a cliff? And I hear they have a bird sanctuary up there too, with a super-impressive raptor show. Eagles, falcons, all that stuff."

"We've got plans already," said Ashley.

Molly couldn't help thinking that if Ryan were still alive, the whole group would be making plans together. But instead they were all unhappily spinning in their separate universes, disordered and grief-stricken.

❧

AFTER TEXTING Ben and asking him to dinner, Molly got into bed, pulled the covers up to her chin, and lay still for a moment. Then she called Lawrence, who was on his usual stool at Chez Papa.

"I was just about to order lunch, my dear," he said. "Come on over! It's such a dreary day and rumor has it the chef is making onion soup. Your stool is warm and waiting for you."

"I just can't," she said weakly.

"If you're refusing onion soup on a day like this, something must be terribly wrong. Tell."

"It's unbelievable. I mean, not literally, it's *believable*, it happens all the time. I've just never...and in this particular case...."

"What, Molly?" Lawrence asked gently.

"Hey, this may be a first—I'm finding out the bad news before you. One of my guests. He was Mr. Happy. Mr. Life of the Party. I found him in the woods hanging from an oak tree."

"God."

"I know."

"How long had he been at La Baraque?"

"Just since Saturday. I know it's only been a few days, but believe me, it's been a very social few days—this group, the biggest I've ever had, had really gelled and they were congregating in my house, carousing and living it up. Everyone really seemed to be enjoying themselves, you know? And this one guy, Ryan Tuck—he was the spirit of the whole thing. A live-for-the-moment sort of guy who looked for joy and found it, even in unlikely places."

"Hmm."

"Onion soup does sound mighty good."

"I could bring you some?"

"Oh, you're sweet, but I'm not an invalid! Just feel like hiding from the world for a little bit. Ben's coming for dinner."

"Ah. Should I ask questions about that?"

"Nah. I'm very glad he's coming, if that's what you're looking for."

"Sort of," said Lawrence, and Molly could hear the smile in his voice. "Listen Molls, the new guy behind the bar is bringing out my soup as we speak, can I call you later?"

"Of course. I think I'm going to take a nap."

"Never thought of you as a napper. Sometimes that can be just the thing. Kisses."

"Back at ya," said Molly, and hung up. And almost immediately she fell into a fitful sleep that lasted for several hours. By the time she woke, there was no time to do any shopping. She trusted she could find something to cobble together for Ben's dinner, and slipped into the fancy shower with all the massaging spray nozzles, using an unconscionable amount of hot water, letting it beat down on her back and head as though the heat and force of the droplets would assuage her sorrow and confusion over Ryan's death.

She put on a little mascara and rubbed some product into her hair so that at least she would look a little more presentable, instead of like something the orange cat dragged in.

"You look wonderful," said Ben when he came in, giving her a peck on both cheeks.

"Can't go wrong, opening with that," she said, smiling. "Though I'll tell you, I'm not going to be the most light-hearted companion tonight. Have you heard?"

Ben nodded. "Maron called. He's gotten into the habit of letting me know when anyone in Castillac dies, for any reason. I guess he thinks the calls are a kind of insurance, like I might prevent him from making some kind of terrible mistake or something." Ben shrugged. "And maybe he's right. It is always good to have the opinion of someone you trust. I don't get the feeling he gets on with Paul-Henri very well."

"Monsour? No," said Molly, not thinking about the gendarmes but of Ryan stuffing three gougères in his mouth at the same time to show her how much he adored them.

Ben watched her. "Ryan Tuck—he's the man who kissed you the other night?" he asked nonchalantly.

Molly quickly looked up and met his eyes. "Yes. I wondered if you saw that. You should know—*please* understand—it meant nothing. From either one of us. He was just...affectionate that way. Impulsive. He wasn't—we weren't at all—"

Ben laughed. "I love that you're worried."

"I'm not worried."

"Okay. Anyway, I was only here for a few minutes that night. It was clear that...how to explain this...I didn't leave in a huff about the kiss or anything else. It was simply that it was obvious the group had a bond and I was an outsider. Like you were all on a kind of journey and I was too far behind to catch up. Does that make sense?"

"Very much so. It's funny you say journey because that's exactly what it felt like. People were talking intensely, laughing like maniacs—you'd have thought it was some kind of reunion of people who knew each other very well a long time ago. Who knows why that kind of thing just happens? But speaking as the host, it felt like magic. Very satisfying to see my guests enjoying themselves so deeply. They are not an easy group, by any means, or people you'd guess would have any particular affinity for one another.

"I keep saying this—but some of what made the fun possible, if not most of it—was Ryan. He cheered up people like Darcy, who has barely said a civil word to me since she got here. I think nerdy Nathaniel thought he'd made a new best friend. Ashley seemed to have a crush on him. He was the center of the whole thing. It's just...just really, really heartbreaking."

"Is it possible that his good spirits might have been a sort of giddiness that was the product of knowing he didn't have much time left?"

"What are you saying?"

"Well, the way you describe him, he seems almost too fun-loving to be real. Like a magical elf or something, bringing people together under a spell. And I can think of some circumstances in which that might make sense. For instance—what if he had recently gotten terrible news from a doctor? A fatal diagnosis of some condition that would be an agonizing way to die? Many would consider suicide in such a case, and I certainly wouldn't judge them for it."

Molly leaned her elbows on the counter and thought about that. "He seemed very healthy, though."

"But you know that kind of impression can be deceiving."

"That's a big part of what's bothering me, to be completely honest. I know it's making this tragic thing all about me, but I can't help feeling like Ryan duped me, and the rest of the guests. If he was that miserable—or facing some terrible end, like you say —why not share it?"

"Do you really not understand that? Some people are not built for sharing, like you are, Molly. Some people can only manage difficult things by keeping them private.

Molly gave a short nod. Though Ben was right, she did not really understand. "Well, all I'm saying is that I think there's at least some possibility that he did not kill himself."

Ben cocked his head and waited for her to elaborate. Instead she went to the refrigerator and began to ramble on about how little was in there for them to have for dinner.

"What do you mean, he didn't kill himself? You're saying someone else killed him, and staged it to look like suicide?"

"Yes. That's exactly what I'm saying." Ben rolled his eyes but Molly was in the pantry and did not see. "Do you like canned sausages and lentils? It's a guilty pleasure of mine. Well, I hope you do, because otherwise the cupboard is bare. I had too much to do on Saturday to go to the market, and here it is Monday and I still haven't gone. And my guests have cleaned me out."

"I love sausage and lentils."

"Excellent. While I heat them up, you can tell me why you think I'm out of my mind and refusing to accept what happened." She dumped the contents of the can into a saucepan and turned on the heat. Then she turned and looked at Ben. He opened his arms and she let herself fall against his chest. He folded his arms around her, and Molly put her head down on his sturdy shoulder and, at long last, let the tears come.

8

It was an early night. Molly told Ben she needed to get to bed extra early, she was feeling so wrung out. Her sleep was fitful, and she woke the next morning feeling as though she had barely slept. La Baraque was quiet except for the intermittent barks of Bobo as she raced around the outside of the house excitedly chasing rabbits. Molly didn't know the habits of her guests yet, which ones got up early and who liked to sleep in. She crept out to the kitchen half expecting to see the whole group in the living room where she'd left them, waiting to be fed and entertained.

She had guzzled her first cup of coffee and was still in her bathrobe when someone knocked on the front door. Expecting one of the guests, Molly was taken aback when she saw that it was Gilles Maron, looking grim-faced.

"Bonjour, Gilles. Sorry about the bathrobe. Is anything the matter?"

"Not going to beat around the bush. I've just heard from Nagrand. Ryan Tuck wasn't a suicide. It was murder."

Molly's hand flew to her mouth. They stood in the doorway letting gusts of cold air sweep into the house.

"So let's get the I-told-you-so's out of the way straight off," he said, squaring his shoulders. "You said it wasn't suicide, and you were correct."

Molly was still standing with her hand over her mouth and the other hand on the door handle, stunned to be proven right. "What did Nagrand say?"

"In his inimitable way, he mocked the murderer for choosing hanging, because, according to him, a hanging death produces very clear signs in the corpse that are impossible to reproduce by other means. He says any coroner worth his salt would be able to tell that Tuck did not die by hanging. Though I suspect in part that is Nagrand's way of giving himself a compliment, which is not unusual for him."

Molly's mind was racing. "You did just say murder?"

"Yes, Molly. Murder. By garrotte, apparently. He did have marks on the neck, so at the scene there was nothing that looked suspicious. Only according to Nagrand, they were not the right sort of marks."

"Garrotte! So...that would point toward a premeditated act, wouldn't it? Does Nagrand know what was used? Wire, cord, rope?"

"You don't waste any time, do you, Molly?" Maron said.

"Well, yes, actually," she said, a bit snappishly. "It's two days after the murder and we're just now starting to call it that. So I'd say there's been considerable waste of very valuable time so far." She didn't usually let anyone get to her like that, but she couldn't help resenting the implication that all she cared about was getting on a case. Perhaps resenting it especially because it was a little bit true.

Molly finally closed the front door, though now the entire downstairs of her house was freezing. "Listen, Gilles, would you give me five minutes to throw on some clothes? Is it all right if I call Ben?"

"No on both counts. This is an investigation of the Castillac gendarmerie," he said. "I'm here not for a consultation but an interview. I'm going to need to talk to all of your guests, and I have already put in the paperwork to see if I can hold them all here in the village until some progress is made on the case. And I do not have time to wait around while you make yourself presentable, just sit down here—do you have any source of heat? It's arctic in here—and allow me to begin."

Molly sagged into a chair by the stove, her plan to take a gigantic mug of coffee back to bed fizzling, but also curious to find out what else Maron knew.

"Since you called it as murder two days ago," he continued, "you must have given some thought to who might have reason to kill Tuck? I'm playing catch-up here, but it certainly seems as though the murderer is most likely staying here at La Baraque. Wouldn't you say so, Madame Sutton?"

"Love how you call me 'madame' when you want to get all official," scoffed Molly, peeved that he would not allow her to get dressed. "As for the identity of the murderer, yes, I have given it a bit of thought, but I'm sorry to say I haven't gotten anywhere at all. I suppose we always have the Random Psycho Stranger theory to fall back on, but that's almost never correct, is it?"

"Your *guests*, Molly."

"You can understand the many reasons I am not delighted to go in that direction?"

"You as much as anyone know it's not me choosing the direction. It's the facts of the case."

Molly drew in a lungful of air and held her breath for a moment, trying to pull herself together. Maron was right. Ryan had been murdered in the woods behind La Baraque. The chance was infinitesimally small that he had somehow met up with a murderous stranger late at night on the outskirts of Castillac and allowed himself to be lured into the woods and done in. While Ryan was no bodybuilder, he looked to have been in decent shape, not someone easily overcome. Far more likely he died because he trusted whomever he was in the woods with, and so the murderer had gotten the significant advantage of surprise.

"Death by garrotte—it's pretty quick, isn't it?" asked Molly.

"Yes," said Maron, though he had no idea. He made a mental note to Google it when he had the chance.

Using a tape recorder as well as a pad and pen, Maron took extensive notes as Molly went through the recent days' events. Who had arrived when, their movements (as best as she could remember), and their reasons for coming to Castillac. He asked who had had a substantial amount of conversation with Tuck, which made her laugh out loud.

"You don't understand, the answer to that is *everyone*. It's a very convivial group. They get along like..." She searched for a French version of "gangbusters" but came up empty.

"All right. Was there anyone in particular that he talked to more than the others?"

"Me," Molly blurted out. "Maybe Ashley? I wasn't with them every second. On Sunday night I was the first one to go to bed, so I have no idea who stayed up or what they talked about. I did wake and hear music at one point."

"What kind?"

"Jazz. On someone's phone, probably. I'm not a fan of jazz so I put my pillow over my head and went back to sleep."

Maron looked at her as though she had just announced she ate live worms for breakfast every morning. "What kind of person doesn't like jazz? Especially an American!"

"We're not all the same, you know."

"Madame Sutton, please remember this is a murder investigation and a formal interview. It's awkward since we are acquainted but please, since there's no getting around that, please confine your remarks to the matter at hand and what I specifically ask you."

"Yes, Chief," she said, maintaining a respectful expression with some effort, and resisting the urge to salute, while pointing out that he had been the one to veer off the subject.

"Would you call Tuck's behavior flirtatious?"

Molly looked out of the window and did not answer immediately.

Bingo, thought Maron, smiling to himself. "Was he flirtatious with you?"

"You Frenchmen think you've cornered the market on charm," Molly shot back.

"I'll mark that down as a 'yes.'"

"Oh, come on, Gilles. Okay, he was a teeny little bit flirty with me. And with Darcy and Ashley, hell, probably with all the women here. But it was...well, it was sort of French, really, now that I think of it. He wasn't really putting the moves on me. More just showing his appreciation. You know? Making a connection. It was part of enjoying life, not about serious seduction or anything like that."

"And do you know that it was the same with the others, or are you guessing?"

"I have no idea. Darcy is married...oh, so is that where you're going with this? Jealous husband?"

Maron made an exaggerated Gallic shrug. "It is the first minutes of the investigation, Molly. I am not 'going' anywhere at all. Merely trying to assemble as much information as I can about what went on over the last few days, before it disappears into the mists of memory."

"That's very poetic."

"I am French, after all. In case it has slipped your mind."

Molly guffawed and then pulled her bathrobe tighter. She would almost have thought Maron was flirting with her, except she knew that was an impossibility given their history. That, and the complete absence of attraction on either side.

"Please elaborate on Tuck and Madame..." Maron consulted

his notes, "...Bilson? Darcy, married to Ira Bilson, is that correct? How serious was Tuck's flirting with her?"

"Well, let's see...there was a moment last night, when Ashley had gotten everyone belly dancing. They were a bit tipsy from champagne, and I did see Ryan dancing with Darcy. He had his hands on her hips as she swiveled them in a figure-eight, sort of dancing with her while she was belly dancing."

"Belly dancing?"

"Ah, yeah, it was harmless enough. Just something silly they were doing. They didn't seem to mind looking foolish in front of each other. Which was especially remarkable given how prickly some members of the group are."

"Prickly?" Molly had used the French word for "spiky" and Maron was confused.

"Darcy takes offense very easily. Ashley gets headaches. Patty likes to gossip. Ira is a doormat with a temper. Nathaniel seems sad. They are not, taken one by one, a fun-loving, easygoing group."

"Interesting," said Maron.

"Maybe," said Molly. For as sure as she had been about Ryan's not having killed himself, she was utterly at sea about where to look for his killer.

Perhaps thanks to Ryan's influence, ironically enough, she liked all her guests. Even the spiky ones.

❧

After another forty-five minutes of going over the same ground, Maron finally asked where he could find the guests, but when Molly walked him around La Baraque they found not a soul. Since the guests seemed to have scattered for the day, Maron took off for the station. Molly, hungry and exhausted, took a large mug of coffee and a plate of buttered toast with gooseberry jam and climbed into bed, still wearing her bathrobe. There was so much to do; but at the moment, she felt talked out and tired down to her marrow.

Gooseberry jam, just by itself, would be reason enough to move to France, she thought, closing her eyes as she chewed so that all her attention could focus on the rich, fruity taste.

She had polished off one piece of toast and opened her tablet to read when Bobo, who had been lying pressed to Molly's side, lifted her head toward the door. Molly heard footsteps scurry closer, then silence. Bobo whined. Someone was waiting in the corridor outside her bedroom.

Molly knew she should get up. But her legs felt leaden and she just could not make herself do it. "Yes?" she called out. "Do you need something?"

In an instant Patty was at the side of the bed. "Hi Molly," she said brightly. "I admit, I was sort of trying to listen in the hallway while you talked to that policeman. So, uh, wow! Murder!"

"I'm afraid so," said Molly. Their eyes met and they saw that they were both glad, perhaps for different reasons. "Listen, Patty, I don't want this to sound at all rude, but I have to ask you not to come inside my house like this without knocking. It's not about you, please understand—just a rule I have in place for all my guests. I'm sure you understand, with me being a woman living alone and all." One of the things Molly had loved about Castillac was the fact that no one locked their doors, but maybe it was time to reconsider that policy.

"Whatever you say," said Patty, but Molly was not sure what she said had sunk in. "So, you guys talked for a very long time! You're friends with the cop and all? I hope that means he's going to keep you up to date on whatever evidence he gathers. As you can imagine, Ashley is taking this whole thing very, very hard. And so anything I can find out and tell her, it would be a comfort. She's going to be a wreck when she finds out the latest."

"Patty, Chief Maron is not going to be sharing that kind of information with me. I'm sorry, that's just not how it works. It's not like this is happening on a television show. There are legal procedures that must be followed."

Patty did not seem to hear. "I've never been part of a murder investigation before," Patty continued. "Do you mind if I have a seat? When is the cop coming back to talk to us? Should we go to the station and make an appointment?" She started to lower herself to the edge of Molly's bed but Molly looked so aghast that Patty stood back up again.

Molly sipped her coffee slowly. She wanted the young woman to go away and leave her in peace, but she managed to keep that from showing in her expression. "I'm sorry. I can't answer any of your questions. I'm sure Chief Maron will be in touch."

"I can't imagine there's too much going on in Castillac that will slow him down. Maybe he'll come back later today?"

Molly shrugged and took another sip. "You know, when I first met you, I thought you were quite shy," she said to Patty.

"I *am* shy."

"Really."

"Well, I'm not shy here at La Baraque, because we've spent time together. We've shared something, been through something together. And you—I feel like I know you, Molly. Like we've been friends for a long time or something."

Molly smiled faintly, admitting to herself that she felt a little the same way about Patty.

"Anyway, I was doing some thinking out in the hallway, and a couple of things sort of stick out, if you know what I mean."

Molly's ears pricked up, just barely. "Stick out?"

"Well, for one thing, Ryan's a guy, obviously, and not a weakling. So there's no way any of the women could have killed him. I'm assuming, of course, that the murderer is one of us here at La Baraque? I mean, maybe it's possible that he pissed someone off in Castillac. But I'm going with the high-probability options first."

Molly just looked at Patty and blinked. She felt so very tired.

"Just to be thorough, I include you on the list of suspects, but like I say, the murderer is unlikely to be female so you get crossed off right away." Patty smiled as though Molly should feeling ever so grateful for the exculpatory strike.

"Thank you very much," murmured Molly. "And have you narrowed things down from there?"

Patty shrugged. "It's early days. But I did want to share...not the kind of thing I would ever tell anyone, under normal circumstances, but this isn't normal, is it?"

Molly bit the corner off the second piece of toast, aware that it was rude to eat without offering her guest anything, and then took another bite. It tasted a little funny, like the jam had gone off somehow, although she hadn't noticed anything with the first piece of toast.

Patty rolled up the sleeves of her shirt. She was wearing jeans that Molly thought might have been purchased in the children's department, she was that small.

"What I want to tell you is, on the first night we were here, on Saturday? I overheard Darcy saying some really harsh things to Ira. They were over in the corner of the room, where she keeps doing those blasted headstands? You were in the kitchen with Ryan, and everyone else was around the woodstove. And, I don't know, it looked like they were arguing...so I sidled over to hear what they were saying."

Eavesdropping was one of Molly's favorite sports, and yet, she noticed that when someone else did it, the practice seemed just a tad distasteful.

"And so I didn't catch every word," Patty continued, "but she was telling him to lay off the pastries because he already had a butt the size of a barn."

"Oh my."

"I know, right?"

"What did Ira say?"

"It was sad to see, it really was. He just hung his head like

Darcy had slapped him. He didn't say anything back that I could hear. Not long after that, they left."

"So what are you...are you implying that Darcy...?"

"Nope," said Patty quickly. "Just thought you'd be interested."

"Thank you," said Molly, her eyelids feeling as though they had weights on them. "I don't mean to be abrupt, Patty, but for some reason—maybe it's everything that's happened—I am just exhausted. I'm going to try to get a little more sleep, if you don't mind."

"You can go back to sleep after drinking all that coffee? My mother always said it was the devil's beverage. She was some serious about church, my mother!" Patty eased herself down on the corner of the bed and laughed. "We weren't allowed to dance, play cards, drink coffee...Oh, the list of sins was pretty much *endless."*

Molly was baffled. Had she been unclear about wanting Patty to go?

"...and this one time, my older brother wanted to go to a barn dance. The most innocent thing you can imagine. Just a banjo and a guitar player, and some square dancing. You'd have thought he had asked if he could go on a date with Satan himself!"

"Patty. Let's continue this conversation a little later, after I've had some more rest. Goodbye for now!" and with that, Molly flopped on her side and closed her eyes.

Patty stood up but didn't leave right away. She waited a long moment to see if Molly's eyes would open again. But eventually she gave up and crept out of the room, and Molly fell into a deep slumber.

9

Patty returned to her room just long enough to drop the bombshell on Ashley.

"Hey, are you ever getting out of bed?" she said, giving her friend a slap on the arm.

Ashley was sitting in bed with a laptop open, several pillows fluffed up behind her and the luxurious comforter pulled up to her waist. "I'm doing a bit of shopping," she said. "I'm absolutely undone about Ryan. I don't think I'll ever get over it."

"Ash, you just met the guy."

"Have you never heard of *coup de foudre?*"

"Since I speak no French except for 'bonjour,' no, I have never heard of cooda foodruh." Patty rolled her eyes.

"It means lightning bolt. As in love at first sight."

"That's just great. In love with a dead guy." Patty shook her head. "Listen, I've got news. While everyone else is moping around feeling sorry for themselves, I've been doing my best to find out what's really going on around here. Hold on to your hat, Miss Ashley Gander. If I really believed you were as fragile as you like to make out, I might not even tell you. But I guess it'll get out anyway."

"What'll get out?" asked Ashley, perking up in spite of herself.

"Ryan Tuck did not kill himself."

"Of course he didn't."

Patty stared. "So...you do understand what that means?"

"I never for one single solitary moment thought that charming man would do himself in. He was positively electrifying, Patty, are you blind? Too lively, too gay!"

Patty raised her eyebrows.

"Not that kind of gay," snapped Ashley. "We had a spark, Ryan and I. Couldn't you see it? Didn't *everyone* see it?"

Patty narrowed her eyes at her friend. Had Ashley really not noticed that Ryan had been flirting with everyone, not just her? "Look, Ash, you don't seem to be following your idea to its conclusion. If Ryan didn't kill himself, what does that mean?"

Ashley looked at her blankly.

"How did he end up dead, hanging from a rope?" Patty almost shouted, exasperated.

Ashley's hand flew to her mouth as she gasped. "Someone killed him?" she whispered.

Patty grinned and nodded. "Now you're getting it," she said. "Not only that—someone here, at La Baraque."

Ashley's eyes widened.

"Maybe it was you," said Patty sarcastically. "So listen, are you getting up or not? I want to go into Castillac and have a real look around. It's too cold to walk and the village looks super cute. Are you coming, or were you planning on spending your vacation doing stuff you could do in your own bed back in Charleston."

"Go on without me," murmured Ashley, letting her head fall back on the pillow. "How could anyone...."

"Umm," said Patty. "Ryan was a flirt and probably a jerk. I never bought his act for one second. But if you want to lie around and moon over some fantasy, then I'll leave you to it." She put on a wool cap and scarf, slipped on her coat, and closed the door behind her.

I love Patty, truly I do, thought Ashley. But great heavens above, she can be such a tyrant when she gets in a mood.

Ashley got up from bed and stood in front of the full-length mirror on the door of the armoire, turning to the side, then looking at herself over her shoulder, imagining she was in a photo shoot for French Vogue. She lifted the hem of her frilly nightgown for a view of her legs, changed her pose, then let the nightgown drop.

Molly had intended this room to be specifically for women travelers of a particular type, and had equipped it with a gorgeous vanity with an enormous mirror. Ashley sat on the pale green velvet seat and studied her face, trying different angles; smiling, then looking serious, then sorrowful. She rooted around in her makeup bag and went through a long process of wiping her face with individual moist towelettes to clean and then tone her skin. Next, she applied a creamy foundation. Then she drew on dramatic eyeliner and wiped it off. She put dark shadow on her eyelids, which made her eyes look sultry and a little spooky. More eyeliner, many layers of mascara.

With the help of more moist towelettes, the mascara came off and false eyelashes went on.

Blush. Lip liner. Lipstick.

When her face was finished, Ashley stood up from the makeup table and opened the armoire. In the bottom sat Patty's small duffel. An under-packer, Patty had brought what Ashley would consider inadequate for an overnight, much less ten days of overseas travel. Ashley found an inner pocket and reached in for the wallet she had seen Patty stash there, and flipped it open.

Her friend had diligently saved for the trip over the course of a year. All her spending money—except what she had taken to the village that morning—was in the wallet. Ashley cocked her head, pursed her lips, and took out a hundred euros. Carefully, she put the wallet back and zipped the duffel, tucking the money into one of her own bags.

Then she sat back down on the green velvet seat, looked at herself in the mirror, and began to cry.

❧

"BUT CONSTANCE, it's so late in the day. The doctor's not going to see patients unless it's an emergency, right?"

"Nah, he sees people when they're sick, Molls! It's not like a big city here, remember? And if you don't mind my saying, you look like crap."

"Thank you."

"And see? You're all touchy. Not yourself."

Molly heaved a big sigh. Usually she felt energetic enough—tired when it was bedtime, but not during the day—not if she had gotten enough sleep. But recently... "All I did was walk into the village and back," she admitted. "And it feels like I scaled Mount Everest. My legs ache and I want to take a nap."

"Not yourself," repeated Constance. She took out her cell and tapped in Dr. Vernay's number. "Usually, a new murder would have you skipping around like you won the lottery."

"You make me sound like a monster."

"Well, you sort of are. A zombie, I guess, or some ghoul that feeds on death. Something along those lines," Constance said, thinking it over.

"You've been playing video games with Thomas again, haven't you?" Molly said weakly.

"Yes, and it's fun, so hush. The doc's phone's busy, so let's just get over there in person. Sometimes he makes house calls, but you're not quite that bad off, are you? You can manage a trip to his office?"

"Of course I can," Molly said irritably. She sat up and put on a pair of low boots, but didn't stand up. "I'm just so deadly tired. What's that a symptom of?"

"Pretty much everything."

Molly sighed. They got moving, if slowly, and for the first time Molly let Constance drive the Citroën. Constance turned out to be a careful and competent driver. Molly leaned her head against the window and closed her eyes, still enjoying the newness and soft leather seats, and trying to concentrate on that instead of on how shaky she felt.

"Bonjour, Constance," said a woman in a thick gray sweater as she opened the front door to the doctor's house. "I hope you are well?" she said as they kissed cheeks.

"Right as rain! It's my friend here who's not so hot. Robinette Vernay, this is Molly Sutton, she lives—"

"Molly Sutton! Of course I know who you are! I am an old friend of Valerie Boutillier. Gerard delivered her, of course. You are an absolute hero to half this village, I hope you know that."

Molly smiled, appreciative. But she was already tired just from the effort of getting there.

"Dr. Vernay is nearly done, if you could just wait five or ten minutes. Can you tell me what seems to be the trouble?"

"Fatigue. From doing nothing."

"Oh, I wouldn't say that, Molls! You've got six, no five guests at La Baraque at the moment, plus a heaping helping of drama. She's so modest. Not the braggy type," Constance said to Robinette.

The woman took Molly's pulse and gave her a long, appraising look. "Well, deep fatigue—could be cancer. Or any of the neurological diseases. Gerard will have to see."

Molly looked at her in horror.

"Robinette!" Constance laughed. "She's not a doctor or a nurse, Molly, but the doctor's wife. And she's known for being the most pessimistic person on the planet. The Voice of Doom, always."

Robinette smiled while raking her fingers through her shoulder-length dark brown hair. "It is good to expect the worst. Then you have no surprises. And if things turn out well, then..."

She swept her hand out as though gesturing to something wonderful.

"Then you've wasted all kinds of time living in fear and misery!" said Constance, still amused.

Robinette excused herself and left Constance and Molly in the waiting room, which was a small salon on one side of the downstairs hall.

"Do doctors all have their offices in their houses?" asked Molly. "You never, ever see this in the States. It might not even be legal."

Constance widened her eyes. "Not legal? How weird. There are modern offices here too, but especially village doctors—they often see patients in a part of their house. For them it's obviously much cheaper than renting an office, and it's nice for the patients too. Homey, not so sterile, you know?"

"Sterile's maybe not such a bad thing when you're sick," murmured Molly. But looking around the small room, at the dark oil paintings in gilt frames that would never grace an American doctor's office, a taxidermied civet on top of a console table covered with bibelots, and a pile of Turkish carpets on the parquet floor, she admitted that visually it was far more interesting than the bland sort of decoration you'd see in a doctor's office back home. She had the feeling that even without having met him, she knew something of the doctor's character. She managed to get up to look more closely at a painting of an elephant with shirtless men grouped around the animal's front legs, when the doctor himself entered the room.

Constance made introductions. The doctor kept his eyes on Molly's as he took her hands in his, expressing his regret that she wasn't feeling well, and asked if she would like to be examined.

"Yes," said Molly. "Please. And then wave your magic wand and make me myself again."

The doctor nodded with a wry smile. Constance waited in the salon while Molly disappeared into the examining room. Apparently, it was expected she would remove her clothes without being given a gown to put on, but Molly didn't care. She trusted this doctor with the painting of an elephant in his waiting room. His manner was professional, and he exuded a kind of goodwill that made her believe she was in good hands. She noted the intensity of his curiosity as he tried to determine what was causing her symptoms.

"It's a bit like solving mysteries, being a doctor, isn't it," she said, as she lay on her back and he palpated her abdomen.

Dr. Vernay nodded, but his ear was cocked toward her belly and he listened while thumping different parts of it. He took her pulse again, asked her to sit up, took the pulse, then to stand, and took it a fourth time. He went through a long list of questions about her symptoms, habits, diet.

"Do you go in the forest much?" he asked finally.

Molly nodded. "I like to walk. When I discovered the trails and the trail maps available at the *Presse*, I was in heaven! And I have a dog who of course loves to go on a walk in the woods more than anything on this earth."

"Have you noticed any rashes? Do you check for ticks when you come out of the woods?"

Molly slowly shook her head. "Are you saying...Lyme disease?"

"Possibly," said the doctor. "Unfortunately, we do not have an especially accurate test for it, in my opinion. So I tend to use the following strategy: I will give you some doses meant to kill the bacteria, and if you then feel ill, we will know it is working, and that indeed you are infected. You might already know that when people speak of 'Lyme' they are usually simplifying: any number of tick-borne diseases likely to have infected a person who has borreliosis, the specific infection of Lyme disease."

"Sorry, my brain doesn't seem to be working that well, either. Can you back up? Did you just say you were going to give me something to make me feel worse?"

"I did," said Dr. Vernay. "In the short term. You will feel worse because your body will be flooded with dead bacteria, and it's quite toxic. Your body may or may not be able to deal with that efficiently. People are different."

"Uff. That is not good news."

"I'm afraid it is not. But you say you've only been tired quite recently. So the infection, even if originally contracted sometime in the past, has only recently begun to tax you unduly. My prognosis for you is entirely optimistic. A few weeks of discomfort, six weeks or two months of treatment, depending on how you do, and all will be well."

Molly heaved another sigh. "Thank you. I hope so."

"Feeling depressed is not at all unusual. It is very difficult, emotionally, to have our energy and vitality taken away from us."

"I'll say."

"I prescribe exercise, but only as tolerated. Do not push yourself. Eat plenty of soup. Perhaps save sweets for after you are well."

"No sweets?"

"Not if you wish to get well quickly."

"Do you have to deliver that kind of bad news all day long?"

"Often. But also I deliver a lot of babies, so it all evens out."

When they were back in the car, Constance offered to drive around to Pâtisserie Bujold, thinking to cheer Molly up. But the patient, on that very first day of treatment, held fast to doctor's orders, and instead Constance took her home and tucked her into bed with a mug of green tea, and then, without asking Molly, she called Ben to let him know.

You have to give him a chance to do the right thing, Constance was thinking. And then, her Good Samaritan duties accomplished, Constance scrambled home to the apartment where she lived with Thomas, excited to dive back into the video game they had been playing, while Molly drifted into a fitful sleep.

10

That afternoon, when she didn't see Molly anywhere, Patty made the rounds of all the guestrooms at La Baraque, asking the occupants if they'd like to attend a short memorial for Ryan later that night. First she knocked on the door of the cottage where the Bilsons were staying.

"Come in!" boomed Ira.

Patty came in to see Darcy standing on her head and Ira flopped on the sofa reading a newspaper. "Hey, sorry to bust in on you, but Ashley and I want to have a little service for Ryan and wondered if you'd like to be part of it."

"A service?" said Darcy, her feet dropping to the floor. "We're atheists. Why do you have to bring religion into it?"

"I'm not—it's—nothing is decided or anything. All we want to do is get everyone together to remember him, however you'd like to do that."

"Of course we'd like to be there," said Ira. "What time and where?"

"I thought you were all 'let's move on'?" said Patty.

Ira shrugged. "I am. But maybe some people need to have a

ceremony before they can do that." He pointedly did not look in his wife's direction.

"Nice dragon," said Patty, pointing to the tattoo on Darcy's shoulder after she had dropped out of the headstand and come over. Darcy did not respond but picked up a shirt that had been thrown over the back of the sofa to put on over her tank top. "Um, how about we meet in Molly's living room at nine? Does that give you enough time to have dinner first?"

"Make it ten," said Darcy.

"Fine, see you then."

Next, Patty went back to the guest wing of the main house and knocked on Nathaniel's door.

"So, we're doing a memorial for Ryan tonight. Would you like to come?"

Nathaniel smiled sadly. "Such a horrible thing," he said. "Of course I'll be there. Can I bring anything?"

"Oh, that's a thought. How about a good bottle of whatever you like to drink? Maybe Ashley and I can go to a bakery and bring some little cakes or something? We're thinking ten o'clock, so everyone will have eaten."

"Sure. Yes. Isn't it funny how we all somehow got to La Baraque and have ended up as friends?"

"I know!" said Patty. "Really unusual. Well, I'd guess it is, I can't say I've actually traveled that much before this."

"Me neither," said Nathaniel. "Okay, well, see you later then?"

Patty nodded. She thought for a moment, standing in the hallway; she wasn't in the mood to hang around the room with Ashley, listening to her endless moaning about the spark she'd had with Ryan.

Patty jammed her hands in her jeans pockets since she hadn't packed gloves, and went back to the pigeonnier and then the cottage, lurking in the shadows, trying to hear what the Bilsons were saying. But the old thick walls of those structures didn't lend themselves to eavesdropping, and eventually she circled back to the main house and found the window to Molly's bedroom.

The light was dim and there was a voile curtain in front of the window, but Patty could make out Molly's shape under the billowing comforter, and Bobo curled up next to her. Patty stood for some time looking in, waiting to see if Molly moved or got up; eventually her hands were too cold to continue so she gently opened the French doors and took a place next to the woodstove in Molly's living room.

❧

BY TEN O'CLOCK, all the guests had arrived. The room was chilly and they crowded around the woodstove. Ira went out to get more wood while Ashley shivered, dramatically chattering her teeth.

"It's not that cold, for God's sake," muttered Patty.

"We're not the same person," said Ashley. "We don't have to react the same way to everything." She sat on the edge of the sofa and put a woolen throw over her knees. "I don't see how Molly can stand it being this cold."

"Spoken as a true lady of the South," said Ira, banging the door shut with his foot as he came in with a gigantic armful of wood. "I'll get this thing fired up quick and we'll be warm as toast in a few minutes. Why don't all of you discuss how you want this memorial to go."

"No religion," said Darcy.

"I don't see why you have to slight Jesus," said Ashley.

"Nobody's slighting anyone," Nathaniel jumped in. "How about we make this simple: a minute or two of silence, followed by anyone who wants to, sharing a memory or something about Ryan?"

"Sounds good," said Ira, jabbing the fire with a poker.

"Are you gonna tell them?" Ashley said to Patty.

"Tell us what?" said Ira. "Can we get this over with? I don't stay up late."

"What is with your moods lately? Five seconds ago you were all enthusiastic about this," said Darcy.

Patty stepped into the middle of their circle. "Listen, before we get started? I've got news," she said, her expression a confused mixture of exhilaration and pretend sadness. "I thought the cop would be back by now and he'd be the one to deliver it. But since he's not, I will. Well, here goes: our friend Ryan didn't kill himself. He was murdered."

"What?" said Nathaniel.

"Are you kidding?" asked Ira.

Darcy looked like she had been slapped. Ashley was used to the idea by then and curled up at one end of the sofa, tucking her feet under her. "I said right from the beginning that he would never have hurt himself. I have a sense about people."

"A sense that if you take off your clothes, they'll be interested?" shot Darcy.

"Darce!" said Ira.

"But so," continued Patty, "I don't know that there's anything for us to do. The cop's on the case and maybe he'll be mad that I told everyone. But I thought you should know. Let's just go ahead with the memorial like we planned."

"Who in the world would want to murder someone like Ryan?" marveled Nathaniel.

"Probably a sociopath. I read an article claiming they're much more prevalent than we realize," said Patty.

"Can we just get on with it?" said Ira.

Patty picked up a bottle and waved it in the air. "Want to open the champagne before or after?"

"Before!"

"After!"

"Like herding cats," Nathaniel muttered.

"I don't want it to seem like we're toasting his death," said Darcy.

"That's very sensitive of you," said Ira, glaring at her.

"Whatever," said Ashley. "Just start the moment of silence, okay?"

All five of them went quiet. Patty put down the champagne, Ashley stopped fidgeting with the throw, and Ira dropped into a chair. They were, for once, silent.

❧

IN BED, Molly woke with a sudden jolt and the sense that she was not alone. Not feeling refreshed by sleep, she got out of bed, thinking she must be crazy because Bobo was fast asleep with her head on the pillow, not barking or growling the way she would if a stranger were in the house. Molly slipped on her bathrobe and made her way to the living room, where she found all of her guests huddled around the woodstove, not saying a word, most with their eyes closed.

"Excuse me?" she said tentatively.

"Oh my heavens," said Ashley, "we forgot to invite Molly! Darlin', would you like to put some clothes on and join us? We're about to talk for a little bit about Ryan. You should be here too. It's so important to heal after all that's happened."

Molly stood, blinking. Why was everyone in her house in the middle of the night? Bobo came in with her tail drooping down, and sat next to Ashley, hoping to get some petting.

"We're having a memorial. Just, um, sharing some memories, that's all. We'd love to have you be part of it," said Patty.

"First—please, I am very accommodating, and if you would like to use my house I'll do everything I can to make it happen. But I want you to ask me first. And use the knocker. Hear what I'm saying?" She looked around at the group, trying to see if they realized they had crossed a line. A few mumbled " sorry Molly" so she continued, "About the memorial...I'd be delighted—well, that's not the right word, is it—I'd be *grateful* to hear what you all have to say. You know I was fond of Ryan too, and it would be lovely—well, that's not it either, but you know what I mean. I would very much like to join you. Can you wait just five minutes for me to get dressed?"

No one objected. Back in her bedroom tugging on a pair of jeans, Molly thought about Maron's insistence that Ryan's murderer was one of her guests. She wished it weren't so, but was objective enough to see Maron's point. Unless Ryan had had the bad luck to stumble upon a random killer in a small village, or had been the target of an expert hit, chances were the killer was here at La Baraque. Was, in fact, one of the five people hanging out in her living room at that very moment.

Molly went into the kitchen for a glass of water, wanting a chance to observe the group before joining it. Nathaniel sat on an ottoman, trying to coax Bobo into coming over. Patty and Ashley were on the sofa, looking glum, not speaking. Ira Bilson fiddled with the stove, and Darcy glared at him.

Spiky does not begin to describe this bunch, thought Molly. She tried to summon up some energy. "Okay then," she said brightly, coming over with her glass of water. "Is someone leading?"

"You do it, Nathaniel," said Patty.

"Okay," he said, looking pleased to be named. "We've done the moment of silence," he told Molly apologetically. "Would you like us to do it again?"

"No, no," said Molly. "I can manage that on my own."

"Okay," said Nathaniel, wiggling his fingers against his thighs. "So now, let's go around the room and give everyone who wants to a chance to say something. Ashley, do you want to start?"

Ashley bowed her head. The woolen throw was pulled up to her neck, covering her body, and the tips of her cowboy boots poked out from the bottom end. When she lifted her head, her perfectly made-up face was composed. "I will tell y'all right now that I feel Ryan Tuck and I were soul mates. It was some kind of crazy luck that brought me all the way here to Castillac so we could meet. Not even luck—magic. The first time I saw him was right here in this living room. He was making you laugh, Darcy, and I didn't even realize just then how difficult that is to do. No offense." Ashley paused and rearranged the throw. Darcy started to say something but closed her mouth again.

"He was a magical spirit in this world, is all I have to say, and I am more sorry than I could ever express that he was taken so soon. I hope whoever did this is caught and put away for eternity. Thank you."

Nathaniel looked a little wet around the eyes. "Thank you, Ashley," he said. "Patty, why don't you go next? We can just go around the circle."

"All right," said Patty, standing up, barely as tall as Nathaniel's elbow. "So you know that first night we were here? I was feeling sorta overwhelmed. Never traveled outside the country before, didn't expect to be thrown in with all these other people. I thought it would just be me and Ash, you know? And we've barely even spoken to each other for about ten years, not since getting out of college. She called me out of the blue and asked me to come on this trip, can you believe that?" Patty laughed and then seemed to recall what she was trying to say. "So that first night, I was kinda huddled in the corner, feeling shy. And here comes Ryan, good-looking Ryan with a twinkle in his eye, and he pays attention to me." She laughed. "He was not a magical spirit, not to me at least. But he was kind-hearted. He gave me a glass of wine and asked me a bunch of questions until I wasn't feeling shy anymore. And so...he was a good guy. Rest in peace, Ryan Tuck."

Others in the group nodded. Ashley and Darcy were sniffling.

"And so that was a big reason that what he told me the next night surprised the heck out of me," Patty continued. Everyone looked up quickly. "I'm talking about the day when we started in on the champagne at lunchtime? I think we were all a little tipsy?"

"Drunk," said Ira.

"Right, well, when you guys took a break from the belly dancing, Ryan came over to me. Just for maybe a minute or two. I think after that, he was in the kitchen with Molly. But in that minute, he told me that the reason he had come to Castillac was that he had done something bad back in the States, and needed to disappear for a while. He made a joke out of it, in a way—saying he really loved champagne and so why not find an out-of-the-way place where he could drink champagne and eat well until the trouble blew over?"

A long, stunned silence.

"I can't believe you're doing this," said Ashley in a low voice.

Patty shrugged but looked chastened, like a child who's just been busted by an older sibling.

"A wonderful man has been murdered, and you want to slander him when he can't even defend himself?"

"I'm just saying what he told me. I don't mean anything by it."

"Just shut up, Patty," said Darcy roughly. "You're always looking to stir the crap. Just shut up about Ryan. You don't know anything about him."

"And you do?" said Ashley, incredulously.

"I don't think this is the time, Darce," said Ira.

"Did he tell you what the bad thing was?" asked Nathaniel.

"Okay, everyone, let's get back to the point of this whole thing," said Molly. "I'll go next. My first clear picture of Ryan was looking out of the window and seeing him throw a stick for Bobo. Bobo was, of course, over the moon—she will keep bringing you sticks into the next century if you let her. Ryan was so patient, he just kept throwing that stick over and over. It's a simple thing, but how can you not love a person who is willing to bring so much joy to a dog?"

"And you were in the kitchen with him a lot, looking pretty chummy," said Patty.

"Shut *up*," said Darcy.

"I'll go next," said Nathaniel quickly. "Ryan and I talked about computers. I know, typical guy conversation. Back home, I work at a hospital, in the IT department. Managing all those files and records, you know? And so that's mainly what we talked about. It was nice of him to ask about my work and he seemed genuinely interested in the challenges of it, which frankly is kind of unusual." Nathaniel bowed his head.

Darcy went to stand in front of the woodstove and faced the group. "Well, I was debating whether or not to say anything. But I'm all about honesty, even if some feelings get hurt. I can't let all this talk from Ashley about soul mates go without saying that Ryan and I...we had...a moment, I guess you could call it..."

"Big whup," muttered Ashley.

Darcy shot her a dark look. "Okay, if you're going to be like that, I'll just come right on out with it. That Sunday night, when we were all still drinking champagne. Ashley was getting everybody to do that tacky belly dancing. And Ryan caught my eye and winked at me. Then he took my hand and led me outside, into the moonlight..." Darcy stopped speaking, lost in the memory, smiling wistfully.

"Sorry, man," said Nathaniel in a low voice to Ira.

"Darcy, I don't think—" said Ira.

"Never mind, I'm done with my turn. It's...it's too private to continue. Sorry Ira," she said, tossing him the crumb of acknowledging she had said something hurtful, even if she had no regret at all about whatever it was she had done.

"You want to say anything, Ira?" asked Nathaniel.

Ira shrugged his massive shoulders, and said no. Everyone awkwardly looked away or down at the floor.

"I'm going to call it a night," said Molly. "Thank you for including me. RIP Ryan."

"RIP Ryan," everyone said.

That was no doubt the most uncomfortable memorial ever, thought Molly, as she sank onto her expensive new mattress.

She was so tired that any fear of a murderer being on her property was downgraded to a minor annoyance. Instead of feeling anxious, she thought about Ryan as she settled under the covers, about how he might have been the most audacious flirt she'd ever met, managing to make almost every woman at La Baraque feel as though he was smitten with her. Whatever else you might say about him, the man had skills.

And she was *dying* to know what the bad thing was he'd come to Castillac to escape, if Patty was telling the truth.

11

Officer Monsour took the call. And since the Chief was out —without even bothering to tell Paul-Henri where he had gone—the responsible thing was to go himself and take down the report. One had to take the initiative if one wanted to advance, that's what Madame Monsour always said.

He met Christophe, the driver of the only taxi in Castillac, at Chez Papa. Paul-Henri looked for Nico behind the bar but instead found a young man he did not know, and gave him a short nod. "Have you seen Christophe?" he asked officiously.

"He's usually at that table in the corner," the bartender said. "Maybe he's out on a call."

A muscle twitched in Paul-Henri's jaw. He had just spoken to the driver five minutes ago, and he had said he was at the bistro. Where in the world had he—

The driver emerged from the backroom, wiping his hands on his jeans. "Ah, Christophe!" said Paul-Henri, as though welcoming him to a soirée. He shook his head and started over. "Thank you for your call, monsieur. The gendarmerie cannot solve crimes without the participation and support of the citizenry."

Christophe looked at him blankly. "I heard about what

happened, the American tourist," he said. "I'd taken him from the station to La Baraque just a few days ago. And so, sometime later, I remembered something. Maybe it's nothing."

"We will be the judge of that."

"All right. Well. Sunday nights are usually pretty slow for me. I get a flurry of business on Sunday afternoon, people have to make the train or whatever, but by evening everyone's pretty much tucked in for the night."

Paul-Henri fidgeted but managed not to shout at him to get to the point.

"So I was on my way here to Chez Papa after giving a ride to Victor Lafont. You know him? Lives way out on the road toward Périgueux. Funny, there was a death at his house last year. Anyway, I dropped Victor off and came back to town. Was thinking about having a bowl of cassoulet and going home. But as I went by La Baraque, I saw something a little unusual." Christophe looked at his fingernails and then scratched at his chin.

"Yes?" said Paul-Henri when the pause became unbearable.

"A guy walking along rue des Chênes. We're talking around nine at night. He was wearing a dark overcoat, and a fedora. Dressed for the city, you know?"

"No, I don't know, Christophe. You must give me more detail. A man walking along the road hardly seems strange."

"I'm telling you, it was strange," Christophe said defensively. "I spend most of my waking hours driving around, Officer Monsour. I know how things look, by and large. I can tell when something is out of place."

"And what is out of place about a man walking down the road in an overcoat? It wasn't the middle of the night. He wasn't carrying a knife dripping with blood or waving around a pistol, am I correct? What did he do that you find worth mentioning?"

"Look, you haven't lived in Castillac all that long, if you'll excuse me. We're a long way from any big cities, you understand? And this man—he was not from around here. He was dressed in a way that caught my eye, that made me suspicious. That's all I know and I'm not saying anything more than that. And when I found out that a murder had occurred not two steps from where I saw this stranger, I thought you should know. That's all."

Paul-Henri stretched his top lip over his teeth and narrowed his eyes at the driver. "Thank you, monsieur, for performing your civic duty so admirably. I will take your report to the Chief and investigate it further."

Christophe nodded, looking irritated, and reached in his pocket and pulled out his beeping phone. "I've got a call. We done here?"

"Indubitably," said Paul-Henri, instantly wishing he had chosen a different word.

❧

THE NEXT MORNING, Molly woke to the excited sound Bobo made when a friend was at the door. She dragged herself out of bed, making no effort to look less bedraggled, and found Lawrence on the doorstep holding a large paper bag.

"My dear," he said, taking her by the shoulders and giving her a firm kiss on each cheek. "Constance called and told me about the Lyme. I'm so sorry! She also told me that Vernay said no sweets. Knowing you, that's worse than the diagnosis. Anyway, I stopped by the *traiteur* and got you a container of chicken soup that feeds six."

"Thanks so much. Listen, would you mind if we talk in my bedroom? I haven't started treatment yet, and I cannot begin to describe how tired I am. Just standing here like this is too much."

"Of course, *chérie!* Do want me to sit with you and regale you with gossip from the village? Or I can heat you up some soup and leave. Whatever you wish."

Molly thought for half a second. "I'll take the soup and the gossip," she said, mustering a smile. "Pans are hanging in the rack overhead. I'll leave you to it."

It was remarkable how delicious her bed looked after only being out of it for five minutes. She climbed back in, arranged her pajamas and fluffed the pillows, and closed her eyes. Good thing I shelled out all that money to spiff up my bedroom, she thought, since it looks like I'm going to be spending quite a lot of time in here.

And then, as though a heavy curtain suddenly fell, she was asleep.

Lawrence came in with a bowl of soup on a tray. "I've missed seeing you at Chez Papa," he said, not realizing she was asleep, and she opened one eye. "I was wondering if you were mad at me for something."

"Never," she murmured.

"Glad to hear it. Can you sit up a bit more? Let me get another pillow. I'm going to get you one of those trays with legs so you don't have to balance it on your lap. The traiteur does charge a bloody fortune, but the food is very good, don't you think? I always run right over there for their chicken soup when I feel a cold coming on."

Molly took a sip and moaned.

"Now, I know what you have is much worse than a cold. But still, your nutrition is very important, as I'm sure Vernay told you. If it's all right with you, I'd like that to be my particular job while we get you through this. I can stop by every day with your meals, and when the traiteur gets tiresome, I can do some cooking myself. Plus I'd be happy to do some shopping in Bergerac just for a little variety. I know there are several places there that have good reputations."

Molly looked at Lawrence for a long moment, into his kind and worried face. Tears started to roll down her cheeks.

"What? Oh, chérie, I didn't mean to upset you! I just want to help. I'm not trying to be pushy or act like you're terribly incapacitated."

"It's not that," Molly whispered. "It's...you've got my back."

"That I do. As you would for me."

Molly nodded as emphatically as she could without knocking over the soup.

"All right then, shall I begin with Lapin?" said Lawrence, settling into a slipper chair covered with a rather sumptuous fabric that Molly had splurged on.

"What mess has he gotten himself into now?"

"Not a mess, exactly, but there has been drama. Lapin—our rumpled, ever-single friend—has found himself a girlfriend."

"Ha! I don't think 'rumpled' is the first adjective I'd have used to describe him. He drove me absolutely crazy when I first moved here."

Lawrence grinned. "Well, you *are* his type. A feisty, well-built redhead—who can blame him?" Molly started to protest but Lawrence jumped in. "Only teasing. He does have a bad record with women. Never knows when to keep his mouth shut."

"It's not just his mouth. He looks at you like he's going to take a knife and fork—"

"I know, Molly, I know. Please, lean back on the pillows. Very nice pillows too, I might add. Are they down?"

"This one is. I also got some memory foam for sleeping."

"And how is it, being so very flush? Has the letdown improved at all? We've never really talked about the big picture. Is it as delicious having all that money as all we poor people think it is?"

"We're not going to talk about it now either, not until you give me all the dirt on Lapin and his girlfriend. Who is she? Do we know her?"

"Her name is Anne-Marie, and she's from Toulouse. It's a long-distance relationship, unfortunately for Lapin. I'm telling you, Chez Papa has been a shadow of its former self, with you barely ever there, Frances and Nico still in the Maldives, and

Lapin flitting off to Toulouse all the time. Even Negronis aren't enough to cheer me up."

"You must have gotten to know the new bartender."

"No, can't say that I have. He's nice enough, but not a talker. Blood from a stone, chatting with that one."

"And..." Molly started to ask about Lawrence's boyfriend, since she couldn't remember the last time she'd seen him.

"Stephan? Long gone. But no worries. It was, blessedly, about as amicable a breakup as one could hope for. One night we looked at each other over a platter of roast duck with new potatoes, and knew it was over."

"No period of heartbreak?"

"A token week of self-pity. That's it."

Molly drank another spoonful of soup and fell back on the pillows. "Sorry. I know I don't seem like myself."

"It's true," said Lawrence, looking at her carefully. "One of the great things about you is your vitality. And...it's rather like your tank is empty. Not the cleverest metaphor, but would you agree?"

Molly nodded. "And the timing is terrible, though of course no time is convenient for falling ill. But I've got five guests, a record number. They're pretty much all high-maintenance. And then..." Their eyes met. Molly looked away laughing. "You know, don't you. About everything. Just like always."

"Well, I wouldn't say *that*," answered Lawrence, looking pleased. "You're the one who actually catches the murderers, so your contribution is obviously worth far more than mine. But yes, I have heard that a guest of yours was killed. And that the killer could be...right here at La Baraque. Again, I don't want to step on your toes or anything, but do you really think it's a good idea for you to stay here, under the circumstances? When you're unwell on top of it?"

Molly chewed her upper lip. "Do you...are you saying you think I'm in actual danger? I know when you say the killer is one of my guests, that sounds pretty bad. But it's looking as though the motive was probably jealousy. Ryan was, well, kind of an operator, and we've got guests who couldn't have appreciated that much. And the women themselves could have gotten carried away —'if I can't have him no one will' kind of thing. Whatever went on that led to Ryan's murder, I don't think it had a thing to do with me. And you know, it didn't even happen on my property. Strictly speaking. It could have been committed by someone else entirely, not one of my guests at all."

"But you don't know that, Molly. Not with any certainty." said Lawrence. "And frankly—though I know this will sting—you're not in top form, ready to work the case. You've got to make your recovery your number one priority. And that means plenty of rest and good food and whatever Vernay has in store for you, which by the way I hear is not exactly a walk in the park."

"Yeah, he mentioned something...about how if the treatment works, it will make me feel terrible."

Lawrence reached for one of Molly's hands and squeezed it. "I am sorry you're going to have to go through that. But don't you agree—you *have* to agree—that going through it with a murderer in the house is possibly asking too much, even for you?"

❧

After Lawrence left, Molly nestled under the covers for a nap, quickly dropping into unconsciousness almost as if she'd been drugged. It seemed as though only ten minutes had passed when she woke to hear her phone buzzing on the bedside table.

"Molly," said Maron. "Paul-Henri and I are standing at your front door. Are you in?"

"Hold on, I'll be right there." She dragged herself to sitting and tried to think about what to put on, but her brain felt impossibly sluggish and the concept of jeans/shirt/socks was too difficult to master. She sat for a moment looking at the floor, listening to Bobo bark.

This is not good.

With extreme effort she got her pajamas off and clothes on, and went to the door with her hair sticking out like a fright wig, matted in back with curls spiraling in all directions.

Maron was taken aback. "Molly," he started, but trailed off.

"Bonjour Gilles, Paul-Henri. Sorry, I'm not feeling well. I'm not sure I can help with whatever it is you want, not right this minute."

Paul-Henri's uniform was turned out to perfection, as it always was: every button shining, every crease sharp. He frowned at Molly's hair while saying bonjour.

"Sorry you're not well. However, I'm here to see your guests," said Maron. "Doubtless I will need to talk to you further, depending on what they have to say, but for now my focus is on them. Are you well enough to gather them together? I do of course need to interview them individually, and Paul-Henri is here to assist, but first I would like to see them in one group."

So once again, for what felt to Molly like the millionth time, the five remaining Valentine's week guests congregated in her living room. They demonstrated the grumpiness that seemed to be their usual state in Ryan's absence, sniping and glaring at one another, but Molly felt too weak to try to untangle what any of it meant, if anything.

"Thank you all for coming," said Maron. Molly noticed that he was a lot more confident than when she had first come to Castillac and he was one of the officers serving under Ben. His investigative abilities still failed to wow her; nevertheless, Maron used to have a wary suspiciousness about him that he had learned to hide pretty well.

Maron glanced at each guest in turn before continuing. "As I'm sure you've heard by now, Ryan Tuck did not commit suicide as we originally believed. The coroner has ruled his death a homicide."

"I've been thinking, it must've taken a couple of guys to get that done," said Ira. "He was reasonably fit. Not like anyone's going to say, 'Hey, sure, put that noose around my neck, that'll be fun!'"

Paul-Henri, thrilled to be able to work the case alongside Maron instead of being sent off on some miserable errand, opened his mouth to correct him. But Maron was ready for it and jostled him hard.

"Chief—" started Paul-Henri, but then realized he shouldn't be giving out any details of the cause of death.

"It may well have been two people," said Maron. "Obviously the investigation is in its earliest stages, and there are, therefore, innumerable questions to be answered."

Molly was skeptical about a two-murderer theory. But it was hard for her to concentrate on what he was saying so she went for a glass of water.

"Some of those questions we hope to answer this morning. The fact is that some person or persons made the decision to end Tuck's life. We do not know if the decision was premeditated, or if the motive was money, jealousy, revenge, or any of the hundreds of reasons people have for killing someone. As you say, Monsieur Bilson, we don't know if there was one killer or more than one.

"I hope it does not inconvenience you too much, but I am going to interview each of you, starting right now. Please, as you are waiting your turn, do not leave this room while the process is carried out. Officer Monsour will stay with you. At this point I cannot force any of you to stay in France, but I urge you to do so until we have made substantial progress on the case, preferably an arrest." He lowered his voice slightly. "I say that as much out of concern for your safety as from a desire to bring the killer to justice. I have not spoken with Madame Sutton about this but I hope she can continue to house you here at La Baraque."

"I'm sorry, I'm a bit foggy and need to check the calendar. But I think that should be fine," said Molly from the kitchen, always pleased to have more bookings but wondering exactly who would be paying for the extra days.

"Excellent. Is there anyone who claims this to be an impossibility? You can all stay for a short while, while we get to the bottom of what happened to Monsieur Tuck?"

The guests looked around at each other, waiting to see what the others would say. The level of tension, already high, had jumped up a notch thanks to Maron's warning. It came out in a variety of fidgeting, lip-chewing, fingernail-biting, and leg-jiggling.

"I guess I can handle another week of croissants. Especially if Molly gives us a discount?" said Ashley, breaking the quiet and trying to smile. The others nodded and shrugged. No one said they could not stay. Well played, Maron, thought Molly.

"The other thing I wish to say to you as a group is this: I ask that you all think hard about the days since you came to La Baraque—what you've observed, what you've noticed about your fellow travelers. It can often be the smallest thing that reveals the identity of a killer. And one last thing, though it doubtless goes without saying: be on your guard. Most probably someone among you is dangerous. Do not forget this." Maron clapped his hands together, causing Ashley to jump.

"Let me start with you," he said, gesturing to her. "What is your name? And Molly, is there a room where I can conduct the interviews with privacy?"

Ashley stood up, bashful, as though she were being asked to dance at the cotillion. She fluttered her eyelashes at Maron and Patty rolled her eyes.

"Honestly, she's not like this at home. At least, not all the time," Patty whispered to Nathaniel, who shrugged.

"I'm sure she's really nervous," he said. "Who wouldn't be, having to go talk to a gendarme all alone? And that dude looks like he means business."

Molly sent them to the unused music room. Because her usual reaction to stress was to think about food, Molly rummaged through the refrigerator looking for something to make for the waiting guests. But she was too tired to whip up any culinary ambition, and ended up passing around a cheese board with some rather tired-looking specimens, and the end of a wild boar salami. As they ate—ravenously—she leaned her elbows on the counter and watched them. It was hard for her to believe any of them was actually a killer, even though she did have some experience with homicidal people who appeared mild-mannered enough on the surface.

She needed to concentrate. To focus her thoughts and impressions. And she would like to do all that with Ben. But at that moment it was all too much, and she slipped away from the group and back into bed, not staying awake long enough to have even one coherent thought.

12

1986

Eight-year-old Ashley was kneeling on the bathroom sink trying to use her mother's curling iron, but the effect was not turning out the way she had envisioned. "Dammit all to hell," she muttered to herself.

"Ashley Gander," said her mother from the next room. "Do I hear you cussin' in there like trailer trash? Did I raise you to talk like that?"

"I'm by myself!" shouted Ashley.

"I don't care if you're standing on top of Mount Everest without a soul to see for miles. You do not use that kind of language in this house. Or anybody else's house for that matter. And you just keep in mind that every single thing you do and say reflects back on me, and I won't have it."

Ashley made a face in the mirror and hopped off the sink. The bathroom was very cramped, so that getting down without banging into anything was something of an athletic feat. "Mama," she said, coming into the living room, "I need some new pants. Mine are too small and they're uncomfortable."

"Tight is trendy, honey darlin'. Look at this magazine right here, what all the girls are wearing."

"Stupid Daddy," said Ashley.

"Ha!" said Mrs. Gander. "Your Daddy is just about the stupidest man on the entire planet Earth, yes indeedy. Didn't get a check this month. Didn't get one last month. I'm afraid your Daddy is what's called an A-number-1 dirtbag deadbeat."

"It's not fair."

"Now where in the world did you ever get the idea anything was supposed to be fair? Not from me. So at least I have the consolation of not having anything turn out to be any different from how I expected," she said to herself.

"Marcia has the best clothes. I swear it's something new every damn week."

Mrs. Gander sighed. "What did I just two seconds ago tell you about your mouth? I will not have a potty-mouth for a daughter, I will tell you that right now. Go on in the bathroom and wash your mouth out with soap."

"Yes, Mama," said Ashley, disappearing into the bathroom again. She stood still in front of the mirror, looking at herself. The she opened her mother's treasured bag of make-up, which she was not allowed to touch under threat of being smacked straight into next week, and took out a lipstick. As carefully as she could, she smoothed it over her thin lips. Then she swept blush over her cheeks and clumsily put mascara on her lashes.

"Oh my goodness, I'm going to be late for work!" cried Mrs. Gander. "I'm running out the door, chile. I'll be back at the usual—"

Ashley heard the flimsy front door bang. They didn't lock up because the lock was broken, and there was no extra money to get it fixed. She put the makeup back in the bag and zipped it up, then wandered into the living room. She was used to being on her own. Her mother worked at the drugstore in their small town, and often babysat after that. She filled a saucepan with water and put it on the stove, then got a box of macaroni and cheese from the cupboard.

If I only had the right clothes, I could run away, she thought, flopping on the sofa. I bet I could be the girl on TV selling cereal. But I can't leave until I get that outfit. At the very least I need those jeans Marcia has.

Back in the bathroom, she turned her face this way and that, made kissy-lips, scowled. She loved the way the makeup made her look like someone else, someone to reckon with. She wondered: when she ran away, would she miss her mother?

No.

She went into the tiny kitchen, climbed up on the counter, and took down the porcelain cookie jar that her mother kept cash in. She knelt down on the counter and looked in at the money, then allowed herself to reach in and take out the bills and lovingly count it. $47. A damn fortune.

13

Back at the station, Maron and Monsour decided to go ahead and discuss the interviews while they were still fresh, rather than waiting until the following day.

"You sure you don't mind?" Maron asked. "It's well past time to go home."

"You're very kind to be so solicitous," said Paul-Henri in that stuffy way that made Maron want to smack him. "I'm prepared to go through the interviews with you now, and there's something else I'd like to bring up that I believe is quite important."

"Yes?" said Maron, stuffing his irritation down out of sight.

"Well, perhaps it is an...awkward thing, given the history of everyone concerned. But if we are filling our list of suspects for the murder of Ryan Tuck with the names of those at La Baraque, based simply on their having the opportunity to have killed him—and I concur one hundred per cent that we should be doing just that—"

"Get to the point," growled Maron.

"Why isn't Molly Sutton on the list?"

"Molly?"

"Yes. She was there. She had opportunity. As of now, unless

you have evidence I have not had the privilege of seeing, she had the same opportunity as anyone else to garrotte Monsieur Tuck."

"We know Molly. She's caught a number of criminals for us, for Christ's sake."

"By that reasoning, if a person once does good, it is impossible for that person to do wrong. I submit that your—"

"Give it a rest, Paul-Henri. We're not putting Molly on the suspect list." He paused. "Not unless some other evidence comes up that gives us a reason to."

"Well," Paul-Henri sniffed, "I'm glad you haven't made up your mind entirely. I would also like to inquire what will be done about the evidence Christophe gave?"

"The taxi driver?"

"Yes. The taxi driver who witnessed a strange man walking down rue des Chênes on the night of the murder. I know I have not been in Castillac long, but it does seem as though February is not a month in which the streets are filled with tourists or strangers or, frankly, much of anyone."

Maron waved his hand dismissively. "Just a man Christophe does not know, walking down the road? That's...that's nothing, Paul-Henri."

"But Christophe—"

"—is not a detective, or a gendarme. With nothing else suspicious, I'm going to ignore it. Of course, if you find out anything else, you are welcome to—"

"Are you telling me to continue following the lead?" Paul-Henri sat up very straight and brushed nonexistent lint off his trousers.

"Okay. Yes. Follow the lead," answered Maron weakly. He sighed, thinking briefly of how much he had enjoyed his job when Ben Dufort was Chief and he and Thérèse were the subordinate officers. Well, he corrected himself—he hadn't actually enjoyed it. But he should have.

"All right, let's get to the guests at La Baraque," he said, straightening a pile of papers on his desk. "First interview, Ashley Gander. Twenty-eight years old. Not the sharpest knife in the drawer. She very nearly made a pass at me."

"Now, that's interesting. Could be a sign of guilt, trying to co-opt the primary investigator."

Maron shrugged. "My impression was that that's how she acts around most anything in trousers. Not that it was specific to me, particularly. However, she did go on at length about her relationship with the deceased. How they had a mystical connection, he was her soul mate, that sort of thing."

"Do you believe her? Is she trying to make it look as though she loved him, so couldn't be the killer?"

Maron shrugged again. "Just let me get through the data and then we can try and sift through it. Anyway, she says she's broken-hearted over his death, hopes we'll catch who did this, etc." Maron looked at his notepad and drummed a pencil on his desk. "As far as movements that night, she says she drank too much champagne, got a headache, and went to bed just after midnight. Says Patty, the woman she's traveling with, will verify this."

Paul-Henri gave a short nod, miffed that Maron was not more interested in either Molly Sutton or the stranger in the dark coat.

"Next was Patty McMahon, Ashley's travel-mate. She's quite petite, looks to be about twelve. I couldn't get a read on her, to be honest. She prattled on about how this was her first trip out of the country and how much she adores France. I was thinking she was mild-mannered and couldn't hurt a fly...and then, not sure why, something turned, like a switch got flipped. She jumped up out of her chair and walked around the room excitedly, telling me snippets of this and that about the other guests.

"Snippets?"

"Oh, innocuous gossip, for the most part, though of course sometimes that sort of thing can be useful. When the group got tipsy, Ashley got everyone belly dancing. Ira Bilson isn't very nice to his wife. Stuff like that."

"Do you think she's telling the truth?"

"Don't know yet. But I think so. Like I said, maybe it will turn out to be helpful at some point. She...she said something about Molly as well, which will please you."

"You misunderstand, Chief. It's not that I want Molly to be guilty, or in any kind of trouble at all. Only thinking we should be thorough and by the book."

Maron understood perfectly well that Molly's success as an amateur detective rankled Paul-Henri to a high degree, but he said nothing about it. "Patty said that Ryan and Molly had been flirting heavily, and that she had seen Ryan kiss her while they were in the kitchen, which as you know is open to the living room."

"Aha!" said Paul-Henri.

"No idea what you're aha-ing about. Apparently Ryan Tuck was quite a player. He managed to get nearly all the women at La Baraque smitten with him at once. Ashley, Molly, and also Darcy, who I'll get to in a moment."

"Everyone except Patty?"

"Hmm."

"Indeed."

"But Patty—no way could she have killed Tuck, not without help. She's a tiny little thing. If she crept up behind you with a garrotte, you'd flick her off easier than swatting a mosquito."

"Maybe she had help then."

"That makes no sense, Paul-Henri. If she wanted to kill him because she felt left out, how is she going to get someone else to do the killing for her? Especially when the guests at La Baraque were strangers when they got to La Baraque? No, I think we can safely cross Patty McMahon off the list. She's sort of an unpleasant person, and she did go to bed later than most of the others so the timing could have worked. But I don't see any way for her to have physically accomplished the deed."

Paul-Henri shrugged, making it clear he did not agree.

"All right, the Bilsons went next, Ira and Darcy. If ever there was an example to prevent you from deciding to marry, this couple would do it. Darcy expressed nothing but contempt for her husband. She also was under Tuck's spell. Said he was the 'embodiment of the light' or some other nonsense. She naturally has a sour expression, but when she spoke of Tuck, her face brightened and she looked like a different person. She—quite forthrightly, I believed—admitted that on the night of the murder, she had too much to drink and had no idea what time she got to bed. Did not remember whether she and her husband had gone to bed at the same time."

"Perhaps she is a blackout drunk?"

"Could be. I can pursue that with her husband in the next round."

"So Ira Bilson—if his wife was that besotted, what did he think of it? Did he admit to any jealousy?"

"Well, they are sort of hippie types. Ira talked a little about free love and following your path. Lost me pretty quickly. So, to answer your question, no, he was rationalizing the situation, and if he did feel jealousy, he was either hiding it from me or from himself."

"Unless he actually believes those things."

"Correct. In my judgment, he does not. No one does. Oh, all right, before you interrupt, sure, there are some people who really do believe in that kind of thing and in my view they're welcome to it. But my sense of Ira Bilson is that he wants to be free-thinking but is, in reality, just as mired in petty emotions as the rest of us. But I make no claim to absolute certainty—we will simply have to watch and see what happens over the next week, and hope the picture becomes clearer."

The two men were quiet, musing over the suspects and the case. Paul-Henri twiddled one of the buttons on his jacket and Maron struggled not to snap at him to quit it.

Maron said, "Oh, I forgot one thing about Darcy. She said she and Ira are hoping to conceive a child while in France. Can you imagine having those two as parents? Anyway, she'd talked about this wish with Ryan, and said he was sympathetic and a good listener. That's probably the main thing I learned about the victim through these interviews: Tuck seems to have been a man who connected with others easily. No one had a bad word to say against him."

Eventually Paul-Henri sighed. "Strange thing about this case. You'd sort of expect the disagreeable person to get strangled, not the one everybody liked."

Maron nodded. "Yes. Well, apparently one person was faking it."

"Unless—"

"Right, the man in the dark coat. *Mon Dieu*, Paul-Henri. Okay, last one, Nathaniel Beech. Back home in Chicago he works in IT at a hospital. Said he was concerned about the women in the group being upset since they had gotten so attached to Tuck. Said that before the murder, they all felt as though the group had made friends for life. Went to bed on the early side, around 10:30."

"Did he seem jealous of all the attention Tuck was getting from the women?"

"Not at all. Told me he has a girlfriend at home and seemed quite enamored of her, wishing she were on the trip, etc. But he is a sensitive sort, and appeared to be genuinely concerned about the feelings of others. Which is a little funny, since I would not say the same about, well, any of the rest."

"A selfish bunch, eh?"

"At first meeting, yes. But we will get to know them better."

"Perhaps I might do several of the interviews?" asked Paul-Henri, trying mightily not to seem overly eager.

"We'll see," said Maron, putting on his coat with a silent sigh.

14

At 9:00 Friday morning, the Bilsons were still in bed, Ira on his laptop, and Darcy just waking up.

"Lovey, what would you like to do for breakfast? Shall we go back to the Café de la Place? I thought the croissants were *impeccable*, as the French say!"

"Ira, must you torture me with your bad French accent?"

"Sorry." He leaned over and kissed the dragon tattoo on her shoulder. "I know you're upset, and when you're upset, you lash out."

"Honestly, Ira, just for once in your life don't say anything annoying!"

Ira took in an enormous amount of air through his nostrils, performing some yogic breathing in order to calm his nervous system, which irritated Darcy even further, but she managed not to comment.

"That's odd," he said, looking at an email.

Darcy flopped over in bed.

"Hmm," said Ira.

Darcy cracked open one eye and then shut it again.

"I wonder if it means anything at all."

"Dammit, Ira!" Darcy swung out of bed and came to look over Ira's shoulder.

"I posted some pictures of the other night on Facebook," he said. "I know some of our friends at home are following along on our trip."

"Why don't you post photos of, I don't know, the Eiffel Tower and stuff like that? You don't need to put up pictures of the people we meet. No one cares about that."

"Oh, my dearest, people do. Take a look at this." Ira clicked to show her the email he had just received, from some good friends back home who were the sort of people who had a million friends from all over:

> The weirdest thing! The guy with his arm around Darcy—he looks exactly like another friend of ours! I mean like total doppelganger! Think you could get his email so I can get them together?

"He's talking about Ryan?" asked Darcy.

"Yes, sweetness, he appears to be the only one with his arm around you," said Ira, a bit drily. "So at least you may be consoled to know that he has a double somewhere out in the world."

"Oh, shut up, Ira. As I'm sure even you could have figured out by now, it was not Ryan's looks that made him attractive. It was his spirit. The good looks, well, that was just a side bonus."

"Right," said Ira, trying and failing to keep a note of bitterness from his voice.

Darcy got out of bed and disappeared into the bathroom without another word.

Ira thought for a moment. Then he opened a new file, and made a list of all the guests at La Baraque. And then—his wife was known for taking endlessly long showers, and this time used up the entire contents of the hot water heater in one shower—he methodically began to Google each name and take notes on what he found. He was a thorough man, good with detail, and he wondered to himself that it had taken him so long to do the sort of research he should have done when the group first starting spending time together.

Always good to know what cards the others are holding, he thought, typing rapidly. And even better if they do not know you know.

❧

WHEN NO ONE answered the door, Ben tried the handle and found it unlocked. He stepped inside the foyer of La Baraque just as Bobo came flying out to greet him, slamming into his legs so hard that a less sturdy man might have been bowled right over.

"I'm glad to see you too, Bobo," laughed Ben. "And where is your mistress?"

"In here!" said Molly, sitting up in bed and raking her fingers through the tornado atop her head.

Ben sat on the side of the bed and leaned in to kiss her. He kissed her on the mouth, and it was not a dry little peck. Not exceedingly amorous either, but warm, and sensual. Molly appreciated it.

"So tell me what Dr. Vernay said? I trust him completely, if that helps. He has an excellent mind and could have had an illustrious career in medicine if he had been willing to leave Castillac."

"You have such a soft spot for this place," said Molly, smiling.

"So it's Lyme? Is that definitive?"

"Not yet. He wanted me to rest up a few days, then the treatment will start. The way he explains it, how the treatment goes will pretty much confirm the diagnosis. Or not. I guess at this point I'm hoping it is Lyme, because if it's not, I'm back to square one. It's horrible to feel this out of it," she added softly.

"I understand," said Ben, brushing her hair back from her face. He had a way of sitting quietly without fidgeting or seeming uncomfortable that made Molly relax. "So, please tell me what I can do for you. Would you like some chicken soup?"

"Lawrence has that covered, thanks. Just your coming over, that's helpful," she said, sinking back into the pillows after a wave of exhaustion crashed over her. Who knew that just having a conversation took so much energy?

Ben watched her face, concerned. "Are you too tired to get up? Would you like to take a walk or something, get a little fresh air?

Molly shook her head.

"Do you feel too crummy to talk business?"

"Never!" said Molly, but her voice was not strong.

"Well, I'm hoping you and I will be able to play a role in the new case. Obviously you're right in the middle of it, and have access to all the suspects...but Molly, I'm afraid, looking at you—and you're lovely as ever, of course—but you do look all in, like you could use a week of solid rest. All I was going to suggest was that you keep socializing with your guests. Keep them talking, keep them interacting. Observe."

"I can do that," she said weakly, but with her eyes closed.

Ben took her hand and watched her fall asleep, feeling concerned but glad she was in the good hands of Dr. Vernay, and thinking she truly was as lovely as ever, though her freckles seemed a bit faded and he would wish for more color in her cheeks. He stayed another ten minutes, until he let go of her hand and it slid down beside her leg on the plush comforter. He crept out without waking her.

❧

WHEN MOLLY WOKE several hours later, she was disappointed that Ben was gone. I barely got a chance to talk to him, she thought. She got up and took a shower, and after getting dressed she sat on the edge of the bed, already wanting to climb back under the covers. But Molly was made of stronger stuff than that.

She forced herself to put on a jacket and scarf and go outside, hoping a short amble around La Baraque in the cool air would help her feel better.

Oh, what I would give for it to be June, and the swimming pool ready to jump into! She gazed at the spot at the bottom of the meadow where the pool was slated to go, looking forward to it with all her heart. She sort of missed having workmen around the place—it gave a sense of pushing forward, improvement, not to mention affording Molly a few more people to talk to.

The pigeonnier was quiet. She wondered whether Ashley's headaches had abated, and if she and Patty were out having a regular sort of touristy day, seeing the sights and eating too much. On her way to the cottage to check on the Bilsons, she tried to focus her mind on the murder. If the killer *was* one of her guests, was there any way to eliminate any of them? Would the Bilsons and Patty and Ashley give alibis for the other person they were staying with, out of loyalty? Was there any chance that any of the guests had known each other before coming to Castillac, but not said anything about it?

How far in advance had the murder been planned? Had it happened because of something Ryan had done, or because the murderer had other motives?

As usual, too many questions and not enough answers. Well, zero answers, but who's counting?

Molly was just about to turn around and go back to the main house when she heard raised voices. As quickly as she could, she moved closer to the cottage, pretending to look at a small bush around the side of the building.

"Ira, just leave it alone, will you?"

"I would very much like to do that, Lovey, but in this case—"

"This case—*bah*. You just want to be the big man, the guy the gendarmes will want to talk to. Has it even occurred to you that if you start telling them stuff like this, it might make *you* look guilty?"

"What are you implying?"

"I'm not implying anything, I'm speaking directly. Your evidence is just a bunch of stupid Facebook gossip and not anything to be taken seriously. But the gendarmes will go deeper than that, Ira. They'll be thinking, okay, why is this guy coming to us and telling us this stuff? Why does anyone want to muddy the investigation, huh? Because he's guilty, that's why. Because he was so jealous of the connection Ryan had with his wife that he wants to discredit him any way he can. As though killing him wasn't enough."

Molly peeked through a crack in the curtains and saw Ira shake his head slowly, but he did not answer. Molly ducked down before either of them spotted her.

"Mark is a good friend of mine, I've known him since we were kids," said Ira. "He's not exactly given to wild theories and imaginative flights of fancy."

"I don't care if he's Albert Einstein."

"Huh? What does that even mean?"

"I'm just saying, your friend can be the most facts-driven person on the planet, and I will not believe him."

"Why does it matter to you, anyway? Oh, right, because you loved Ryan so utterly. Wouldn't want to think anything at all against him, would you?"

"Look, okay," said Darcy, almost sounding conciliatory. "Your friend is probably just mistaken. Easy enough to do. Do not say anything about this, Ira. Not if you want to avoid getting put in a French jail. And I hear they still use leg irons."

"You just made that up."

"Research 'French jail' and see what you find."

Next came a stream of muttering, and Molly moved closer to the window to see if she could hear the rest of what they were saying. But the window was closed and the walls were thick, and unfortunately the Bilsons were now speaking in low voices. Worried about being caught, Molly slipped back to the front of the cottage and down the path, chewing on her lip as she tried to guess what Ira's friend might have told him about Ryan Tuck that Darcy did not like.

He was so cute, Molly thought, remembering how he had kissed her in the kitchen, and for the first time all day, her face had a bit of color.

15

The next morning was a chilly, gray Saturday, and Molly was determined to get to the market since she had missed it the week before. Market day was the best place to get the freshest food, of course—straight from nearby farms. It also happened to offer the freshest gossip from an even wider variety of sources.

As she drank coffee and got Bobo fed, the guests drifted into the living room of La Baraque and peppered Molly with a steady stream of questions: Was there anyplace to get octopus? Could she explain European shoe sizes? Did she know that Castillac had faster internet than Charleston? Had she heard anything from the gendarmes about when they might be able to leave?

"Sorry," said Molly. "I'm afraid I don't know anything more than you do about the investigation or how long they expect it to take. Though I can tell you they likely have no idea, unless there's a heap of evidence they haven't made public."

"I hear you're sort of an honorary gendarme yourself," said Ira, who had found a few mentions of Molly's prowess as a detective on an online expat forum.

"Eh," said Molly with a shrug. She had an urge to tell them about the private investigator business she was starting with Ben, but hadn't quite forgotten that there was a murderer among them. Perhaps she should keep it under her hat a little longer. "Well, I see it's drizzling just a little, but I never let that keep me from the market. Most of the vendors will have awnings or umbrellas up so there are dry spots to dodge in and out of. Anyone want to come with me?"

"If you're sure Chief Maron doesn't want to talk to us, I thought I'd drive over to Montignac and see the cave paintings," said Patty.

"I'd love to see them too! Want some company?" asked Nathaniel.

"Sure," said Patty. "You coming, Ash?"

"I desperately need to go to a beauty store," said Ashley.

"Really," murmured Darcy.

Ashley threw her a sour glance but did not bite.

"I'll go with you," Darcy said to Molly, as though agreeing to punishment. "Ira's been about as much fun as a root canal lately, so it'll be better than nothing."

"Bless you for your enthusiasm!" said Molly, laughing.

Ira went back to the cottage while Ashley convinced Patty to drop her off in Périgueux on the way to Montignac.

"I really like walking in the rain, but maybe it's a little too chilly," said Molly, leading Darcy to the Citroën. "Sorry to ask this again, my brain's been feeling fuzzy lately. Have you been to France before? A French market in particular?"

"No on both counts. When I was maybe sixteen? My father dangled a European trip in front of me, trying to get me to break up with my boyfriend. Didn't work."

"Ah. Likely made you hold on to him tighter?"

"Yup. And the guy was a total dirtbag," said Darcy, smiling at the memory. They drove in silence to the edge of the village, where Molly slowed down to look for a parking spot.

"So, when did you get interested in cheese?" Molly stopped and neatly backed the car into a space barely big enough. The drizzling had stopped, and she and Darcy walked toward the Place with their coat hoods down.

"When I was born," said Darcy. "It was a joke in my family, how I'd sometimes have only cheese for dinner."

"Well then, France is definitely the place for you."

"The cheese *has* been amazing," agreed Darcy. "After Ira and I got together, we started looking around for a different kind of life. We wanted to get out of the city and live more, uh, wholesome, you know? Get some goats and make cheese, was what we decided on. I have about fifteen kinds I want to try." Molly glanced over and saw that the young woman was smiling an authentic smile and for the first time since arriving in Castillac, actually looked happy. And then, before Molly could ask what sorts of cheese she had in mind, Darcy's face fell. "Look," she said, pointing at a mother pushing a baby carriage.

Molly's expression dropped right along with her guest's, though she made an effort to hide it. Her deepest desire was to have a child, and she was acutely aware that at her age, she was running out of time. She knew the mother and stopped to coo over the baby and ask how he was doing. Darcy just stood and stared with her fists clenched at her sides.

"The main market is another few blocks," Molly told her as the mother and baby went in the opposite direction. "Most likely Lela Vidal will be there, and maybe I can show you a few other unusual cheeses that the traveling cheesemonger occasionally has. Until I moved here, I had no idea that cheeses could be seasonal." She could sense a change in Darcy's mood—not difficult since the other woman was glowering and walking with her fists still balled, as if she were hoping for an excuse to hit someone.

"Is something wrong?"

"That *baby*. I think I told you that I hoped to conceive at La Baraque?"

"You did mention it, yes."

"Well, Ira's not...he's...we haven't been getting along. He knows what I want but...."

Molly nodded, unable to find a single appropriate thing to say.

"You know," said Darcy, her face brightening for a moment, "it wouldn't be hard at all to steal a baby. I could have grabbed that kid out of that carriage and made a break for it. That woman would've been so shocked I'd practically be in Paris before she managed to call the cops."

Molly's mouth opened and closed again.

Darcy nodded. "You think I'm joking? Haha, Molly! You want a kid too, right? You gonna try and tell me you've never thought of it? Never thought of just going up to some woman looking all smug with her new baby and just grabbing it and heading for the hills?"

Again Molly opened her mouth but no sound came out. Was she kidding? She had to be kidding...right?

"Show me the cheese," Darcy said next. Molly walked slowly to the corner of the Place where Vidal usually set up. Darcy was exhausting, and she was suddenly out of energy.

"So, I'll leave you to it," said Molly. "I've got some friends here I'd like to talk to, and then I'll be making a stop at Pâtisserie Bujold before I'm ready to head back. You have a working phone? Can we be in touch by text?"

"Ira is obsessed with the internet," Darcy answered, "so yeah, my phone's all set. Just don't spend all morning gabbing."

Molly hurried away, thinking that Darcy Bilson had won the Rudest Guest award, hands down, covering the entire time La Baraque had been open.

"Maron, it's Dufort."

"Bonjour," said Maron warily.

"Just wanted to check in. I was planning to let you know that

Molly and I are going into business together, doing detective work, but it turns out she's got Lyme disease. I'm not sure how long she's going to be out of commission."

"Sorry to hear that," said Maron, and he meant it, although at the same time he couldn't help feeling that with Molly out of the picture, he had a better chance of solving the Tuck mystery himself. A few good cases under his belt and that Paris posting might be his yet.

"We plan to be private investigators. We'll be based in, but of course not limit our work to the village. Or the *département*, for that matter. I expect we'll be working with you from time to time. I look forward to it."

"As do I," said Maron. That he did *not* mean. His interim appointment as chief had finally been made a full appointment, though he still depended on Dufort for help...and resented it.

"Anyway, I've asked Molly to socialize with her guests as much as she is able, but the last time I saw her, she could barely get out of bed. So this go 'round I'm not sure she's going to be as much help as she usually is. How are things on your end? Do you have any leads on possibilities other than the guests at La Baraque?"

"No. If it had happened at a different time of year, then maybe we could consider other tourists. But you know how it is in Castillac in February. Nobody's out much on these cold, gray days. There are barely any tourists at all."

"Only takes one."

"Sure."

"Things with Paul-Henri going okay?"

Maron started to complain about him but caught himself. "Yes. No problems. Look, if there's nothing else? I've got another call coming in—"

"Yep, talk to you later."

Maron pushed the blinking button on his phone. "*Allô*, Chief Maron speaking."

"Bonjour, Chief. This is Charles Brantley, at the American embassy in Paris."

Maron could tell from the man's tone that he was going to say something Maron did not want to hear. His intuition turned out to be entirely correct.

16

1991

Darcy pulled on the black jeans her mother deplored, the ones with the slashed right leg held together with safety pins. She was short and had to roll the legs up. That sort of spoiled the look, but Darcy was unwilling to spend any time hemming them. How she did up her face was more important. She spent a solid half hour with powder, shadow and eyeliner, just to get the goth effect the way she wanted it: her face so pale it nearly glowed, her eyes dark, sunken caverns. She grinned at her reflection and noted with approval that thanks to the makeup, her teeth looked grayish-yellow.

After putting on boots and grabbing her knapsack, she strode to the front door of her family's large Colonial, making no effort to sneak out.

"What do you think you're doing?" her mother said, appearing out of the shadows as Darcy knew she would.

"I'm meeting somebody. See ya."

"Change out of those pants this minute."

"Nope."

Her mother opened her mouth but said nothing. She had been trying to control her wayward teenage daughter for several years, and was acutely aware that she was failing. "Shall I call your father?" she said finally.

"Don't care," said Darcy, and slammed the door behind her. She got on her expensive racing bike and rode down the driveway, through the development, and out toward the shopping center where her friends were waiting.

"Darce," said a lanky boy dressed in black jeans, who had a line of six silver hoops running along the edge of his ear. "What's going on?"

Darcy dropped her bike, letting it clatter on its side, and shrugged. "Nothing," she said. "Like always."

A few of their gang were farther down the sidewalk, in front of a sub shop; the two wandered in their direction. "Hey Darcy," said another girl, who was wearing a long skirt that would barely stay on after she had cut it to ribbons. "Another boring night to get through. I think we should...do something."

Darcy looked at her skeptically.

"I mean...what if we hold up the sub shop?"

The lanky boy laughed. "What are you gonna do, threaten to fart in the store?"

"Shut up, Ken," said Darcy. "I think Ellie might have a good idea for once. I don't know about you guys, but I'm starving. And my parents refuse to give me any money, after what happened last month."

The others nodded solemnly, not wanting to think about all the trouble they'd gotten into for starting a fire in an abandoned garage.

"Just let me do the talking. Come on," said Darcy. She strode into the sub shop, her eyebrows making a deep V, and she snarled to the clean-cut boy behind the counter. "Make us three Italian subs with extra cheese and extra hot peppers, and—"

"I don't really like hot pepp—"

"Shut up, Ellie," snapped Darcy.

"Sure thing," the boy sang out, and got to work on the sandwiches.

The three teenage goths nervously waited. Ken kept flexing his arms and Ellie bit her fingernails.

"Get ready to look threatening," Darcy whispered to Ken. "If he won't give us the subs, you're gonna have to use some muscle,"

"Um, Darce? That's not really my—"

"Here ya go!" said the boy, pushing the three subs onto the counter where they could reach them. He stepped to the cash register and began to ring up the order, but Darcy grabbed all three subs and ran out the door. Ken and Ellie yelped and followed her.

"But—" said the boy behind the counter, who had never had this happen before and could not quite believe it.

"You were awesome," said Ellie, her eyes shining, as they sat down in the scruffy woods behind the shopping center to enjoy their haul.

Darcy could barely take a bite. She walked around the others, watching them, licking her lips, high on the thrill of breaking the law. Maybe she had, at long last, found something she was good at.

17

Ben knocked, then stuck his head in and called for Molly, in a hurry to tell her his news.

"Well, bonjour, Ben!" she said, from a chair next to the woodstove. "I'm glad to see you. Please excuse my not getting up."

"No, no, please stay where you are," said Ben, swooping down to kiss her cheeks, then her mouth. "I hope it's all right that I showed up without any notice. I've just had the most extraordinary phone call from Maron."

"Do tell," said Molly, pulling her blanket up to her chin.

"It's freezing in here. Let me get some wood and jack this fire up a bit first."

"Sure, leave me dangling!"

Ben was out and back from the woodpile quickly, the orange cat weaving through his legs when he came in. He squatted down by the stove, using a poker to get the logs adjusted the way he wanted them. Then he shut the door, opening the intake. "There you go. You want anything? Can I make you some tea or something?"

"Ben! Quit being a nurse and tell me!"

He sat on the sofa and grinned at her. "It was already an interesting case, right? But now a bit more so. Maron got a call from the American embassy in Paris this morning. Turns out that the family of Ryan Tuck claims that Ryan Tuck is alive and well...and not in France."

Molly stared, digesting the information. "Well, it's not that unusual a name. They must have contacted the wrong one."

"The embassy didn't pick random names from the phone book, Molly. The passport has contact information on it. Tuck's sister, apparently."

"Oh."

"She says she saw Tuck a couple of days ago, in Cincinnati... Ohio? Anyway, she's no fan of her brother—said he's a jerk and something of a con man, and who is at the moment lying low to hide from some woman he's ripped off. He hasn't been using the internet because he's worried the woman's hired someone to tail him."

"So, a real prince."

"Yep. But not our prince."

"Wow. I'm...struggling a little here. So Ryan...was somebody else, impersonating Ryan Tuck? Identity theft?"

"Apparently so."

"And does the embassy have any idea who our guy really was?"

"No. It's going to take some collaboration between the embassies and international law enforcement. If the guy has DNA on file, or even a police record somewhere, it should be easy enough. But if not...."

"We might never know."

"That's right."

"And we may never know why he pretended to be Tuck, or why he came to Castillac...." Molly laughed bitterly. "He told me he had chosen La Baraque because it seemed so serene. He wanted to start his first novel here, and he liked that it was simple yet luxurious."

"He was in one of the new rooms?"

Molly nodded. "Yeah. You know, that reminds me...Tuck—or whoever he was—told Patty that he had come to France because he had done something bad back in the States. Apparently he didn't give her any details, though. It's a little unsettling. An imposter, and I fell for his line completely."

"I've been trying to remind you that there is likely a murderer in your house, too, but somehow that doesn't seem to penetrate," Ben muttered.

"It's...it's hard not to wonder whether everything about him was a lie."

Ben struggled to keep his expression free of gloat.

"You think I got sucked in by some sort of con man," said Molly.

"I didn't say that. I didn't even think it. Look, con men are successful because they're good at making people feel a certain way. And you were just being warm and friendly because that's who you are. It's not like you gave him the password to your bank account or anything."

Molly stared at a piece of bark on the rug, trying and failing to make her memories of Ryan fit with these new facts.

"Right?" added Ben.

"Right. But I trusted him. He threw sticks for Bobo, and I let that...I thought, a guy who throws sticks for a dog when no one is looking—that's sort of the definition of a decent person, you know?"

"Of course you feel betrayed. But people are complicated, Molly, as well you know. He—whoever he really was—could have had a soft spot for dogs *and* be up to no good in other areas."

"I would be happier with myself if I hadn't been such a patsy," she said, slumping down in the chair.

"A patsy? Never," said Ben, laughing. "And anyway, he's dead now. It's his killer we need to focus on."

Ben and Molly both looked at the flickering flames through the glass door of the woodstove, thinking. Molly rubbed her face and blinked her eyes, feeling as though her thoughts were slow to form. "I guess I'm ready for another nap, amazing as that sounds. Going to set a record for the week for hours spent unconscious."

"Do you have any rooms available?"

"Two more in the addition. Why?"

Ben put his arm around her while they walked back to her bedroom. "Because I'd like to move in for a little while. Please think about it and don't say no right away. You're in no shape to be alone—" Seeing her face, he changed course. "Okay, listen, just let me stay in the addition so I can do some work while you get back on your feet. I can hang around under the guise of looking after you while you're not well, and at the same time I'll be observing the guests and maybe asking a few nonchalant questions if I get an opening. It's a rare thing that we have a limited pool of suspects, and they're all staying in the same place like this."

He pulled back the covers and Molly climbed in, fully dressed.

"All right," she said, feeling nothing but relief that he was going to come stay. As she closed her eyes, a sort of slideshow of images of Ryan rolled by: Ryan laughing, Ryan stuffing his face with gougères, Ryan in the corner with Darcy, making her throw her head back with laughter.

Was it all a lie? And whatever he was running from—is that why he was killed?

SHE HAD no idea how long she had slept. But the moment Molly's eyes opened, she was determined to get out of bed and do *something*. A murder had taken place, practically in her yard. No way was she was going to nap straight through the investigation and not be part of it.

After putting on a heavy sweater and some slippers that could be worn outside, she decided to check on the guests. She figured the more she could get them one at a time, away from the others, the more she might hear something worth pursuing.

The weather wasn't half bad. Gray as usual, but with a bit of warmth in the air. So it was not surprising that no one answered at the pigeonnier or the cottage. Molly threw a stick for Bobo on the way back to the house. She entered through the back to see if Nathaniel was in. She nodded approvingly at the decoration in the corridor—the sconces she had found at Lapin's shop were just right, and the pale blue of the walls looked luminous in the overcast light coming in through the old leaded window.

She knocked gently, not expecting an answer, and getting none. Everyone is probably doing what they came to France to do, she thought—out seeing the sights and eating good food, tramping on day hikes, shopping. She knocked one last time, a bit harder. The latch gave, opening the door a crack. Molly considered for half a second, and stepped inside.

Nathaniel kept his room neat. That was not a surprise. As far as she could tell, his foremost quality was not wanting to cause a disturbance—he wanted to do the right thing, wanted everything to be all right—and if his room had been messy, it would have seemed out of keeping with her impression of him.

Molly did have some rules concerning the privacy of her guests. Obviously it was necessary for her to go into their rooms from time to time, for various reasons: plumbing events, illness, and once or twice a forgotten wallet that Molly retrieved for a stranded guest. Just as obviously, it would not be right to snoop.

Well, under most circumstances anyway, she told herself, opening the armoire to see a small row of shirts neatly hung. When one of your guests is a killer, doesn't that throw all the rules out of the window? Guardedly, Molly thought, *Yes*.

She was not looking for anything specific. The used garrotte was unlikely to be stashed under anyone's pillow. But she persevered, because you just never knew what small detail would crack a case wide open.

Molly riffled through the paperback book on the bedside table, felt around the inside of his extra pair of shoes, opened the drawers in the desk and bottom of the armoire, but found nothing. On top of the desk was another book, and she picked it up and glanced at it—a technical book about information technology that went right over her head—and then saw a small piece of paper underneath it.

She felt a fleeting stab as she picked it up and began reading. She knew, of course, that she would not like it one bit if someone went into her bedroom and began reading her letters. But the stab didn't slow her down. She felt the electric sensation of knowing she was about to read something momentous.

"Dearest, dearest Miranda," she read. And then let out a sigh. What did I think I was going to find, a note to Ryan saying he was coming to strangle him? I swear this Lyme business has made me simple-minded.

> Dearest, dearest Miranda,
>
> I can't even describe how much I wish you were with me. France is incredible—the people, the food, everything—and it would be so awesome to be experiencing it with you. I know I said I'd made a lot of friends here, and while it's true some of them are women, it's actually hilarious that you would be even a tiny bit jealous. I love you so much, Miranda! You only!!
>
> I've got no idea when I'll be coming home, which is pretty frustrating. The cops (they're called gendarmes here) seem competent so hopefully it might not be too much longer. And you're very sweet to worry about my staying here with a murderer on the loose! If it helps, I'm not worried about that. I'm pretty sure I know who did it, and it's all about romantic jealousy. Not something I'm mixed up with here, because of course my heart belongs to you. I haven't said anything about my suspicions to the cops because I don't have any actual evidence. Just a strong

feeling backed up by a few odd remarks. No doubt they'll be back and maybe I'll talk to them about it then.

Okay, I'm going to go for a walk into the village—which you would *love*—and get some lunch. I've been eating these ham sandwiches on a baguette with butter almost every day. They're so awesome!

I hope you're feeling good and having fun with your girlfriends while I'm away. Never dreamed I would get stuck in France for something like this, but I'll be home soon.

love love love,

your Nathaniel

Molly put the letter back on the desk, feeling relieved. At least the one guest who seems like a nice guy actually is, she thought. Quickly she glanced around to make sure she hadn't left any sign of her snooping, and left the room.

It's only fair that I get into the other rooms as well, she thought, stopping at Ryan's room for moment before heading back to the main house. Everything was just as she and Maron had left it. She had wondered if she would need to mail off a package of his belongings to his family; now they didn't even have an idea who that family might be.

Who *were* you? she said to him, picturing Ryan's open face, his warm smile, and his twinkling eyes. It's so bizarre that I don't even know your real name.

18

"Yoo-hoo!" warbled Constance, after letting herself into La Baraque. She carried a paper bag from the pharmacy, having been in touch with Dr. Vernay's office and filled the prescriptions at the pharmacy for Molly.

"Bonjour, Constance," said Molly from the kitchen. "I bet it's not almond croissants in that bag."

"No madame, it is not. And I can see by the look on your face that you're not to be trusted. You *are* going to take the medicine, aren't you?"

"Dr. Vernay said it will make me feel terrible. And I'm having a good day today, really I am. So, of course I'll be taking the medicine—it would be silly not to! But...not today."

"Molly!"

"Would you be enthusiastic about taking something that was going to make you sick?"

"If it was the only way to get well, yeah! Sorry to be blunt, but you're not right in the head." Constance got a glass from a shelf and filled it with water. "Here you go, now. Drink a little of this." She dumped the bottles onto the counter, all eleven of them, then took a large glass bottle from her purse. "Hm, one thing you gotta give Dr. Vernay, he's very thorough." She began to read the instructions on each bottle, shaking out the dose and putting everything into a saucer.

Molly stood looking like she was riding in a tumbril, heading straight for the guillotine. "Can't we just start tomorrow?" she asked in a small voice.

"No!"

"Did you hear the latest about Ryan Tuck?" Molly asked, hoping in vain to distract her.

"That he was really some other dude? Oh yeah, that was making the rounds last night."

"You already knew?"

"You forgetting that gossip is the major sport here in Castillac?" laughed Constance.

"We might never find out who he really was."

"Or why he was pretending to be someone else. One thing for sure? He was up to no good."

"You don't think it's possible a person could run away and pretend like that for a good reason? Like maybe his life was in danger and some terrible person was after him?"

"Why *would* somebody be after him—he owed money? Revenge for something terrible *he* did? Come on, Molly. People don't steal identities and jump across the ocean for nothing. Whoever that dude was, he was no Prince Charming."

Molly started to protest but changed her mind. "I just realized the most basic thing. Let's say the guy's real name was Dedalus Morton."

"Who names their kid Dedalus?"

"Nobody! I'm just giving him a name to make it easier to talk about. The thing is—we don't know whether the killer was trying to kill Dedalus, in which case he succeeded—or Ryan Tuck, in which case he failed. In other words, was the murderer tricked by the identity switch same as we were?"

"Beats me, Molls. Let's split these pills into a few handfuls, you can't take them all at once. Come on now, down the hatch!" Constance held them out along with the glass of water. "*Mon Dieu*, you are stubborn! Did your mother want to poke her eyes out with forks, raising you?"

"Probably," said Molly distractedly. Defeated, she took the pills and chased them with a long swallow of water. "And...if the murderer *was* fooled, then that means, *obviously*, that he or she had never actually met Dedalus before. Whew—we've got a lot to look into."

Constance shook her head. "Is Larry coming over later with some food? You know, you're normally pale, but at the moment you're positively ghostly. Get back in bed, why don't you? I'm going to straighten up in here for a bit and then take off. Thomas and I are going to the movies tonight."

Molly smiled, but it was clear she was thinking about the case. She barely registered anything Constance said, though in her preoccupation she was least a little more compliant. Constance herded her back into bed and tucked her in. Molly fell back on the pillows with her eyes closed but her mind tearing around, trying to recall the interactions she had witnessed among her guests, any moments that might mean more now than she had thought at the time.

It was surprisingly fatiguing just to lie in bed and think. Her left arm started to twitch. She drank more water but it tasted strange and she put down the glass, feeling something already shifting in her body from the medicine. But before she could make any sense of what, she was, once again, asleep.

AFTER CONSTANCE NEATENED up the kitchen, she wrote Molly a note saying she'd come back tomorrow and do the gîtes. With the guests staying on indefinitely, there was no changeover day for room cleaning. Leaving by the front door, she bumped into Ben on his way in.

"Bonjour, Constance," he said, and they kissed cheeks. "How is the patient?"

"Not patient at all," she laughed. "Asleep, last I looked. Listen, you're going to have to make sure she takes the medicine when she's supposed to. It's like dealing with a stubborn child, I swear. Tried to talk me into starting some other day."

"She expects to feel worse once the treatment starts."

"I know. But duh, no treatment, no getting better."

Ben nodded. "Thanks for your help. Hope we'll see you later."

Constance waved and left. It was Sunday, and Ben almost got himself a beer, but he had asked Maron to come over, and so thought he should wait. The kitchen was clean and the woodbox was full, he noted approvingly. Molly has good friends.

A short rap on the door, and Ben let in Maron.

"I hope you don't mind some talk about work on a Sunday?" Ben asked.

"Since when does a murder investigation pay attention to the days of the week?"

"True enough. Can I get you a beer?"

Maron hesitated, then nodded. Even though it had been well over a year since Dufort had resigned, he had to keep reminding himself that Ben was no longer his boss.

Ben gestured to the chairs and sofa arranged by the woodstove, and went to the refrigerator. He had taken an extra-long run that morning and had been looking forward to a beer ever since stepping out of the shower afterward.

"Well, look Maron, I want to be very clear. I'm well aware that you are the chief now. And that I have no official capacity with regard to this investigation at all. But I also know it's a tricky case, or at least it seems to be thus far, and you're anxious to get a resolution on the books. So I propose simply that Molly and I consult with you. Strictly on an informal basis. I don't like to malign a member of the gendarmerie—and you know I am a great believer in the potential for good training, and the right mentoring, to lift a mediocre officer out of his incompetence—but, just between you and me, I have heard that Paul-Henri is not...not what you might wish for. I mean, as far as having the instincts of a detective. Is that fair to say?"

"I'm not going to comment," said Maron. "Since you have not been hired by anyone involved—that is correct, yes?—then I don't see a problem with some degree of collaboration. It will be strictly informal, of course. And I can't promise that I will divulge everything we uncover, or do it promptly. I must act with propriety, you understand; it wouldn't do at all for the villagers to think I am merely a puppet that you direct from behind the scenes."

"No, Gilles, not at all, and that is not my agenda. I hope you know me well enough to believe that."

"And these conversations...they will remain private?"

"Certainly. Whatever makes you comfortable. And please understand that Molly and I have the highest respect for your work."

Maron nodded, but he did not especially believe that last bit. He appreciated the gesture, however.

"I'm going to see if Molly feels up to joining us," said Dufort, taking a quick pull on his beer before getting up and walking quietly to her bedroom.

Molly was standing in front of the mirror on the door of the armoire, trying to get a comb through her hair.

"Chérie, Maron is here. Do you feel like joining us?"

"To talk about the case?"

Ben nodded.

"Of course I do," she said, grinning and tossing her comb on the bedside table.

"Glad you're feeling a little better," he said softly, as they returned to the living room.

"So, this latest turn of events," said Maron, when they were back and settled into chairs, "does make figuring out what really happened quite a lot more difficult. First of all, we don't know whether the intended victim was Ryan Tuck or the man who was impersonating him."

"Just what I was thinking," murmured Molly.

"Obviously, it's crucial to identify who he actually was, but that is largely out of our hands. I assume the embassy said that the Americans were involved and working on that?" asked Dufort.

"Yes," said Maron. "I have the names of the American contacts. The first pass will be checking for a DNA match."

"Does that mean you took some DNA from the body?" asked Molly.

"Some routine swabs," answered Maron a little defensively.

"You had a sense about it, didn't you?" asked Molly.

Maron shrugged. "Possibly. Just trying to cover all the bases, as I was taught."

"Um, where's Ryan now?"

"Nagrand still has custody of the body. We expected the Tuck family to want him shipped back to the U.S., but now...until we find out who he really is, I expect he'll stay in the morgue. What we can do here, while the Americans do their part, is find out whether any of the guests had a connection to Ryan Tuck before arriving in Castillac—either the actual Ryan Tuck, or the man so far unidentified."

"If they did, they were really good at hiding it," said Molly. "I think I was present when they all met each other. You'll remember that this is a very sociable bunch. They practically moved into my living room on the first day and partied non-stop, at least until Ryan died. I never noticed even the tiniest bit of anything odd during all the introductions and time spent just after meeting. I mean, sure, of course the murderer could be a good actor, and it's true that I wasn't looking for anything, either. But...that would mean *both* Ryan and the killer would have had to be good actors."

"And—we are assuming now that the killer's target was not 'Ryan Tuck' but the man impersonating him—"

"I've started calling him Dedalus," said Molly.

"Huh?" said Maron.

"Well, he's not Ryan Tuck after all. He needed a new name just for ease of conversation."

"Right, okay. So let's say that the killer somehow finds out Dedalus is coming to La Baraque, follows him here, and while waiting to make his move, pretends not to know him so no one will see they're connected. Why in the world would Dedalus do the same, especially when he would likely have some idea that the killer meant him harm? Why would they both simultaneously agree not to admit they knew each other?" asked Ben.

"And...if the killer had managed to follow 'Ryan Tuck' here, only to arrive and find that the person wasn't Ryan Tuck at all but some stranger—why not call him out, since the murder was off anyway?" asked Molly.

"Because the murderer was hiding his connection with Tuck, not advertising it," said Maron. "Presumably he wouldn't be giving up the whole idea just because the plan to kill him in Castillac didn't work out."

"Right, sorry. It's so complicated!"

A long silence as all three detectives considered how much they did not know, and tried to formulate ways to fill in some of the gaps.

"And what about other leads? Constance told me Christophe is talking all over town about a man in a fedora, walking down rue des Chênes the night of the murder?"

"Red herring," said Maron. "Or at least, nothing further to go on."

"I don't like thinking of that man—Dedalus—lying in the morgue all this time," said Molly. "What happens if we never figure out who he really is?"

"I'm not sure Nagrand has ever had that problem. But I'm

sure there's a protocol somewhere," answered Maron. "All right then. The situation may look more complicated with this stolen identity element added in. And I won't deny that it is. But the best thing is just to treat it as new information, and consider it progress. Unless the killer was fooled by the impersonation—which seems far less likely—I believe we can assume that the target of the murder was indeed Dedalus. Once we have a name, and a profile, I don't think it will be that hard to link him to one of the guests. In the meantime, Molly, say nothing to them about this latest development. Not until we're ready."

"I agree about the target being Dedalus," said Ben. "I haven't interviewed them, of course, but to my eye none of them look like contract killers. The motive for the murder was probably something personal, which means the murderer and the victim knew each other. I know," he added quickly, turning to Molly, "you said you hadn't noticed anything between Dedalus and the others. But perhaps each wanted to keep the association a secret for different reasons. And we have no idea what Dedalus might have been doing in an effort to protect himself. Perhaps all the socializing was simply a strategy—stay in a crowd as much as possible, get the others on his side in case there was a confrontation."

"I see your point," Molly said. "I'm just...as I've said before, the others are not exactly an easygoing bunch. They're difficult and some are even downright unpleasant. But at the same time, they're all just like people you've known all your life, you know? Annoying, hard to get along with maybe, imperfect certainly...but capable of murder? Hard to believe."

"It so often is, even when you have proof," said Ben.

Molly thought of past cases, and nodded ruefully.

19

The next morning, the Bilsons left for Lela Vidal's farm, for an all-day cheese-making workshop. Constance took the opportunity to tidy up the cottage a bit, although without Molly to oversee her work, the place was unlikely to end up dramatically cleaner. Constance had a way of rearranging dirt, Molly sometimes told her, which was not exactly the point of housekeeping. But slowly, the younger woman was improving under Molly's tutelage in the ways of the mop.

Constance had a key to all the gîtes and she let herself in, hoping the Bilsons would prove to be on the neat side. She was quickly disappointed. Empty mugs sat on the coffee table and dirty dishes covered the dining table. A jumble of clothing was wadded up in a corner of the sofa, magazines on the floor, empty potato chip bags underfoot...a real mess. With a sigh (and a grumble), she got a bag from under the sink and started by collecting the trash on the floor. Then she headed into the bedroom to pick up empty cookie packages and soda cans, and from there to the bathroom for more of the same.

I'm no neat freak, she thought, but this is insane. How can they stand to live like this?

Once the trash was off the bathroom floor, she decided to clean since she was already there. A quick scrub to the toilet, spray and wipe down the shower. The area around the sink was cluttered with all kinds of stuff, and she had to move it in order to wipe the surface. Bottles of shampoo, makeup, toothpaste, toothbrushes, combs, hair product—Constance had not met the Bilsons, but imagined they must be very glamorous, considering the number of products they used to make themselves look good. She looked closely at a mascara and some face powder, interested in American cosmetics that couldn't be found in Castillac.

The last remaining object on the counter was a small leather case, a shaving kit, the kind that opens when you squeeze the ends and snaps shut when you squeeze in the other direction. Not the most agile of cleaners, Constance knocked the kit onto the floor as she was getting out a rag, and it popped open—spilling out several hypodermic needles.

Constance frowned. She squatted down and picked one of the needles up. It looked new, unused. She looked inside the kit and found a short length of rubber hose, a spoon, and a small plastic bag of white powder.

Holy smokes, she thought, quickly shoving everything back in the kit. She gave the counter a wipe, put everything back without attempting to make any order out of it, and ran back to the main house to tell Molly.

20

Luckily for the Bilsons, the other attendees at the cheese-making workshop were British. Accordingly, Lela spoke English, though her accent was heavy and occasionally, they couldn't understand exactly what she was saying.

"I don't know why people learn another language and then don't bother to find out how to pronounce it," Darcy muttered under her breath, loud enough for another attendee, Alice Bagley, to hear.

"Sorry if she's using English on my account," the young British woman apologized. "I did take French in school but I'm absolute rubbish at it."

"What? Oh, I don't speak French either," said Darcy, and Alice widened her eyes slightly, but said nothing more.

"The first step in making *cabécou* is to mix this morning's milk with yesterday's, and bring the temperature to ten degrees."

"You freeze it?" Ira whispered.

"Centigrade, you mule," hissed Darcy.

"Now, stir in the whey and rennet, and cheese-making is done for the day," said Lela. "Let's go out to the barn and I'll talk about caring for your herd. Everyone: it is dairy goats, yes? Not the cow?"

"Right, not *the cow,*" said Darcy.

"Darce," said Ira quietly.

"Shut up Ira," she shot back.

"Goats, they are the most amusing of the animals," said Lela, patting a pregnant Alpine on her flank. "By reputation, quite stubborn. Their habits and desires can seem odd while you are getting to know them. For example, very much they like to be high up, so if you do not want them on the roof of your car, make certain to pay good attention to your fencing. I myself use portable electric fence. It is easy to move about and not too expensive to run as the voltage is low. If you have some areas on your property with some difficulties—I mean plants that you would rather to disappear, such as poison ivy as you have in the United States—put the goats to work and they will eat everything right down to the ground."

"Do we have to worry about poisonous plants?" asked Alice, who had moved to the other side of the group, away from Darcy.

"Oh yes!" said Lela. "In fact, it would take several days to go through all the dangers. People think goats are garbage eaters, yes? And they are helpful to eat down plants where you do not want them. But at the same time, you must learn what they cannot absolutely eat. Wild cherries, for example. They can poison a goat quickly and fatally. Certain grasses, especially after a frost, can kill a goat. I have prepared a list for you and I suggest you spend some time in your pasture making sure you know what grows there."

"This is such a big responsibility," said Alice, and Lela agreed.

The group broke for a simple lunch of bread, salami, and cheese, which Lela provided. Ira had brought Cokes for him and Darcy; most of the other attendees drank bottled water, and one older man offered to share a bottle of Pécharmant. The group talked amiably of their herds and cheese-making ambitions, until an argument broke out between Darcy and Alice over whose country's cheese was superior.

"You've got cheddar, I'll give you that," said Darcy to the young Brit. "But come on, you have to admit that overall, the French have you beat by a mile. Your blues don't come anywhere close. Blue Wensleydale? Please." She rolled her eyes.

"You're forgetting Stilton," said Alice, and Darcy's smirk dropped, as she had indeed forgotten Stilton.

"I don't understand why you have to turn it into a competition," said an older woman from Liverpool. "Cheese is cheese. We love to eat it, we want to make it. That's all that matters."

"Hear, hear," said the man who had brought wine.

"You're defensive because, well, *American* cheese?" said Alice. "It's rather an embarrassment, isn't it."

"Oh shut up," said Darcy.

"Darce," said Ira, warningly.

"You can shut up too!" she said, standing up suddenly, and then taking the edge of the table in her hands and flipping it over. Cheese flew up and landed on the floor, the people on the other side of the table were splashed by drinks, but at least no one was hurt when the heavy table fell on its side.

"Pardon," said Lela, who had seen what happened as she was coming into the room with a platter of fruit. "What are you thinking? Madame Bilson, I'm afraid you must leave. I...I have no understanding of your problem. But this...this is not..." she tried to say more but could not find the words in French, much less English. "Go!" she said, pointing at the front door.

Ira started to try to convince her to let them stay, but seeing Lela's expression decided chances were too slim to bother. "Come on," he said, taking his wife's arm. Darcy wrenched away from him and got through the door ahead of him, shouting obscenities at the group and at Lela.

"And your cheese is totally overrated!" was her final attempt at an insult, as Ira caught up to her and the door slammed behind them.

❧

MOLLY SAT on the edge of her bed with her elbows on her knees, trying to decide if she needed to run to the bathroom and throw up. The queasy feeling had started when she took her medicine that morning—a fluorescent yellow, vile-tasting liquid—and her stomach had heaved as it went down. Since then, she had broken into a violent sweat, had tingling pain up and down one arm, and had teetered all day on the verge of vomiting.

Constance knocked lightly on her bedroom door. "Molls? Sorry to be a bother. But can I talk to you for just a sec?"

"Come on in."

"Oh jeez, you look like crap!"

Molly nodded. "I feel more awful than I look, if you can believe it."

"So sorry! I guess Dr. Vernay was right about things getting worse before they get better, huh? At least he's been right so far and probably Lyme is the right diagnosis?"

"I'm not really capable of feeling glad about anything at the moment," Molly said quietly.

"Understood. Jeez! Can I do anything? Run you a bath maybe?"

"Actually, that sounds sort of appealing," said Molly.

"Okay!" Constance ducked into the bathroom and got the bath going, set out a big fluffy towel, and was quickly back at Molly's side. "Not sure if you're feeling too bad for a little tidbit I have for you?"

"What kind of tidbit?" Molly said, lifting her eyes from the floor for the first time.

"Information, not chocolate. Well, you know I was just cleaning up the cottage this morning while the Bilsons are at that cheese thing. You know anything about running a dairy? 'Cause I can tell you, they are not the right people for that line of work. You have to keep everything clean as a whistle, you know? Sanitation is the name of the game in the dairy world! And the Bilsons, oh my—they're a pair of slobs! Trash all over the floor like they don't know what a trashcan is for!"

"Is that the tidbit?"

"No, no! I mean, it's not irrelevant, is it, but I've got something better." Constance wanted to prolong the suspense but could see Molly was in no shape for games. "I found a needle kit in the bathroom."

"A what?"

"Needle kit, Molly. For shooting drugs."

Molly ran a hand through her hair. "Drugs? Needles? You're telling me the Bilsons are shooting drugs?"

"Well, one of them is. Horse, is my guess."

Molly laughed in spite of herself. "*Horse*? Do you get your American slang from '70s movies?" She giggled and then lay back on the bed.

"Okay, heroin then. There was a little packet of it in the kit, too."

"Packet of horse?" Molly said, erupting in laughter.

"You don't think this is a big deal? I do, Molly! People who smuggle drugs overseas are shady characters, if you ask me."

"You think this ties in with Ryan's murder?"

"I don't know...you're the detective! I'm just giving you some information that I happen to think is valuable, and you're finding it hilarious for some reason. It's not going to be any laughing matter when you have an overdose on your hands. You could probably get arrested for having that stuff on your property."

"Okay, okay, I *am* taking this seriously," said Molly, a wave of queasiness putting an end to her amusement. "But look, the needles could be for any number of things. Diabetes. Infertility.

Even vitamin injections. So I wouldn't jump to any conclusions. But...thanks for telling me."

Constance huffily went to the bathroom to check the tub, and announced that it was ready. "I guess I'll go see if I can get into the pigeonnier next. But it'll take another good hour in the cottage to make it fit for human habitation."

"Don't be rifling through their belongings, Constance," Molly warned. "We could both end up in massive trouble for something like that."

"I was just cleaning the bathroom," Constance protested. "The shaving kit fell on the floor and needles spilled out. It wasn't like I was pawing through their stuff."

"Of course, if you happen to notice anything..." whispered Molly, and winked.

Constance winked back, and left to finish up at the cottage while Molly stripped and sank into the hot water. The tub was ancient and huge—so long that she could stretch her legs out and fully submerge.

So one (or both) of the Bilsons might be a drug user, she mused. Might explain some of the mood swings. Though to be precise, Darcy's mood seemed to swing only one way....

❧

"LOVEY," said Ira, as he and Darcy got into the car to leave Lela Vidal's farm.

"Don't start," shot Darcy. "Just for once don't say a word, Ira. I know I messed that up. I know it, okay? But that stupid Alice Bagley pushed me over the edge! How could she bring up American cheese right in front of Lela Vidal? Why did she want to humiliate me like that?"

"I don't think she—"

"Shut *up*, Ira! Just drive. Sometimes I want to have that farm all by myself, just be me and the goats. Because people suck."

Ira sighed. "Would it cheer you up if I told you some of the things I've found out about the others?"

"You mean the people you thought were your new best friends?"

Ira sighed. "We were all having fun, those first days, you included. But the murder does change things, wouldn't you agree?"

"I don't know, does it? Yeah, okay, it means one of us is a violent backstabbing cretin. But that's only one out of five, right? Only one person is guilty, unless you're about to tell me you've uncovered a conspiracy, Mr. Google?"

"Well, I did find out something fairly suspicious. Shocking, even." He waited, hoping she would ask for more, but Darcy said nothing. "If you know your way around a computer," he added, "you can find out pretty much anything about anyone...as long as they've spent some time online."

Still not a word from Darcy.

"Would it surprise you to learn that someone at La Baraque knew Ryan from before?"

"Well, duh, Ira. I didn't think he convinced somebody to murder him in just a few days. Somebody must have followed him here."

"You don't know that. *I* could have killed him for flirting with you so shamelessly."

"But you didn't. You hate confrontation. Plus, you're a sniveling coward."

"Such sweet talk," said Ira, shaking his head. "Listen, Ryan and Ashley knew each other in the States. In fact, they used to be a couple. So put that in your pipe and smoke it."

Darcy glared at Ira. "Ashley?" she spat. "He would never..."

"Oh, but he did. I found a couple of articles in a Charleston paper. Ashley likes high society, I guess. Her name is all over the internet, volunteering for this or that committee of the Junior League, or going to this or that swanky charity fundraiser. And who was her date, on more than one occasion? None other than Ryan Tuck."

"I don't believe it. Why didn't they say anything about knowing each other?"

"I have no idea. I guess they had their reasons."

"Were there photographs? Because I want a photo or it didn't happen."

"Just be on your guard, Lovey. We know Ashley kept a big secret from everyone. Who knows what else she might be hiding?"

"Are you trying to say you've solved the big mystery all by yourself? Jesus Christ, Ira. Quit trying to be a hero."

"You *are* in a mood. Since when do you stick up for people? Especially people I don't have the impression you like very much."

"His murderer could be any of us, Ira. It could be *you.* It could even be me," she added, her voice breaking. Darcy turned her face to the window and would not say anything more.

21

1985

"What is *wrong* with you?" Mrs. Bilson said to her young son Ira, who stood by in agony as his mother read his latest unimpressive report card. "You certainly didn't inherit my brains. Look at this—a C- in history! You don't have to be a genius to do well in third grade history! Just draw a few maps, for heaven's sake."

"I'm not a good drawer," Ira said, though he knew it would only increase his mother's contempt.

"Well, why not?" she snapped. "I'll tell you why. All you do is stay in your room doing nothing, that's why. How do you expect to learn anything that way? Oh, your father is not going to be happy to see this." She shook the paper in his face. "Not happy at all."

Ira looked at his mother as though he were listening, but in his head, he was counting up by prime numbers. He'd gotten to 131 when he noticed she had not said anything for a few minutes, then he scuttled away to his room and closed the door. For his birthday his parents had given him a Nintendo, and he dropped his backpack on the floor, hopped into a beanbag chair, and began to play Super Mario Brothers. The background tune of the game was like a sedative, calming his body from the effects of his mother's harsh words.

Hours passed.

It was dark out and Ira wondered if his mother was making dinner. Sometimes she did, and sometimes she stayed in her room with the door locked. Ira had no idea what she did in there. He didn't like to think about it. His father spent long hours at the office, and usually Ira was in bed before he came home. Mostly, it was just Ira and his mother, alone together in mutual misery.

He crept out of his room, alert for any signs that would tell him how his mother was doing. Had she been going to the liquor cabinet in the dining room? It always smelled funny in there, a mixture of sweet and astringent, with an overlay of tobacco—a smell that made him feel sick to his stomach.

"Ira?" she called from the living room.

He inhaled a quick breath and walked toward her. "Coming, Mom."

Mrs. Bilson was sprawled across the sofa, one leg up over the back. "I think it's time to celebrate," she said, slurring her words. "Call and order Chinessh food. And sit down with me and tell me a sshtory. Entertain me, little man."

"Which do you want me to do first, Mom?"

Mrs. Bilson took a long sip of her drink and then tried to focus her gaze on her son. "Just do it all," she said. "I have to tell you how to do everything?"

Ira quickly went into the hallway where the phone was and looked in a drawer for Chinese takeout menus. He had learned by now that it was better just to pick out whatever he wanted, making sure to get shrimp toast because his mother was slightly obsessed with it, and ask no questions. The Chinese place knew Ira and had the Bilson's MasterCard on file.

"Okay, Mom. They said half an hour."

"Half an *hour?* Do they not understand we are *starving* here?" She threw her head back and laughed. Ira laughed too, but his eyes were flat. "Now, come sit," she said, gesturing to a spot on the sofa next to her.

He moved slowly. He did not want to sit next to her.

"Ira!"

"Coming, Mom."

"Why don't you get your history book and read to me out of it? You go get it and I'll just refresh my drink. You have no idea the week I've had."

Ira scampered upstairs, wishing he could stay in his room until the food came but not daring to. Back in the living room, he sat in a chair across from his mother and began to read aloud about the Pilgrims.

"You do understand that it's nothing but propaganda, that book," his mother interrupted after a few minutes.

"What's poppagander?"

"Lies. Bull. They're trying to make it like the Pilgrims were terrific, but they weren't really. Nobody tells the truth these days." Mrs. Bilson let her head drop and put her hands over her face. Ira knew that tears were on the way. With Mrs. Bilson, tears—and cruelty—were always on the way.

"Should I keep reading?"

"No! Just shut up, Ira!" his mother said, jumping up from the sofa and coming toward him. "Why do have to be so...why are you...what is *wrong* with you?"

Please let the delivery man come, thought Ira. When she got this bad, the arrival of shrimp toast was his only hope.

22

That afternoon, when all the guests had returned to La Baraque from their various touristic endeavors, they wandered around the property, aimless and ill at ease.

"You know, I've been thinking," said Ira, talking to a group on the terrace. "I bet everyone booked their time at La Baraque as a kind of Valentine's Day thing, right? Or, well, at least some of us did. And with all that's happened, Valentine's Day went by without anybody even mentioning it."

"Because it's a stupid commercial holiday that nobody cares about," muttered Darcy.

"So—" said Ira, pressing on, "I know it's awkward, with the investigation and all—but I propose we have a belated Valentine's party. Nothing fancy, just a way to do something positive in spite of this whole mess."

"I can't believe you're suggesting we have a *party,*" said Ashley. "Ryan is dead. One of us is a murderer. Frankly, it gives me the heebie-jeebies to continue staying here. Who knows which one of us might be lurking around after dark, up to no good?"

"Ash," said Patty in a low voice.

"Well, nobody's forcing you to stay. You could pack up and leave at any time," said Darcy.

"And have the gendarmes immediately on my tail? I don't think so," Ashley sneered. "Besides, who gets an excuse to stay in France an extra week or two? I can't pass that up."

"I'm not that concerned either," said Ira. "I mean, unless we're dealing with a serial killer, I don't see how any of us has anything to worry about. Whatever beef the killer had with Ryan was between them." He was careful not to look in Ashley's direction. "Come on, what do you say, everyone? Valentine's party? Who's in?"

"I am, I guess," said Nathaniel. "Obviously everything has changed and there's no getting back to where we were. But it's worth a shot. Ryan would probably be all for it. And besides, no matter what Chief Maron seems to think, I don't see how he can say one hundred percent that the guilty party is one of us. Random murders *do* happen, even in places as charming as Castillac."

"That's the truth," said Darcy. She was watching Ashley's every move, trying to decide whether she believed the other woman had actually been together with Ryan back in the States. "I've been wondering if we should ask Molly for a refund. I mean, we didn't exactly pay all this money to end up as murder suspects with maybe our lives in danger."

"Not a bad idea for once," said Ashley.

Constance was just coming outside, having gotten Ben's room in order, and heard that last bit. "A refund?" she shouted. "After everything Molly has done for you? She could have kicked you all out, you know. You could be staying someplace with scratchy sheets and rats! But she's still welcoming. To *all* of you. Against the advice of her friends, I don't mind saying.

"And let me tell you something else. Perhaps you don't realize that Molly is famous in the village? That she is one of the foremost detectives in all of France, known also for her amazing culinary soirées? In fact, we've got a television producer coming next week to talk about doing a reality show here at La Baraque. That's right," she said, seeing the guests' wide eyes. "A reality show, right here. Guests coming and going, local color, the odd murder—it would be a smash hit!"

"TV?" said Ashley, sitting up straight and posing for an unseen camera.

"A refund is silly," said Nathaniel. "Even if our vacations have taken an unexpected turn—something we'd never have chosen, obviously—it was hardly Molly's fault, what happened."

"One other thing," said Constance, "I'm sure she would rather I didn't say anything...but I'm grabbing hold of the steering wheel here at La Baraque right now, because Molly's been diagnosed with Lyme disease. She's just started the treatment and from all accounts it can be kind of brutal. So please, have some consideration. If you want to leave La Baraque, and France, that's between you and Chief Maron. But if you want to ask Molly for a refund you're going to have to fight your way past me first."

Ira chuckled, looking at spindly Constance standing in the middle of room in a posture of defiance, ready to take on all comers. He was six-foot-five and could have picked Constance up with one hand as easily as a kitten.

"No refund," said Patty, looking down at the floor. "Anyway, I think we signed some kind of disclaimer when we confirmed our reservations. And since we'll be here a little longer, I'm willing to try to make the best of it. I'll come to the party, Ira."

The others all agreed to attend as well, with varying degrees of enthusiasm. Constance nodded approvingly and said goodbye, Bobo trotted back to Molly, and the guests were left on their own to figure out what to do with themselves.

ASHLEY ANNOUNCED she had a splitting headache and was going

to the pigeonnier to lie down. Darcy said she was going for a walk in the woods, alone. Ira went back to the cottage and settled in for another session of Googling.

That left Nathaniel and Patty, both naturally shy. Despite having already spent a day together seeing the cave paintings in Montignac, they looked at each other awkwardly. "Well, do you..." started Patty, "do you want to do something?"

"How about we walk into Castillac and go to a café?" said Nathaniel. "I'm not really all that interested in more sight-seeing, to be honest. Seems like people like to go to famous places just to be able to take a picture and say they saw it."

"I know what you mean," said Patty. "Yeah, sure. Let me get my coat and I'll meet you out front."

Nathaniel was tall and slim, wearing a camel's hair coat that had belonged to his father and was too big for him. Patty looked like a sprite next to him, in her bright green cap and sneakers, walking with a bouncy step and barely as high as his elbow.

"This whole thing is crazy," she said to him, with an air of confidence now that they had a plan and were on their way. "First of all, I thought I was coming on a trip with my sorority sister, and it was just gonna be the two of us, running around eating a lot of French food and seeing a château or two. And instead it turns into a non-stop party with a bunch of strangers with a murder thrown into the mix."

Nathaniel laughed, "I hear you. I planned the trip a long time ago, before I got together with my girlfriend. She couldn't get out of work to join me, so, eh, I wasn't all that excited to be here, you know? I didn't want to waste my money and not come at all. But I sure never expected anything like this."

"So, just between us, who do you think...?"

"Is the killer? I'm *so* glad you asked that. I've been really wondering what everyone is thinking, but no one has the courage to ask. You've got some impressive qualities, Patty McMahon."

Patty shrugged but couldn't help beaming.

Nathaniel jammed his gloveless hands into his pockets. "Well, I'd have to say I just don't know. What motivates a killer? Greed? Passion? Ashley was half in love with him, seemed like. Same with Darcy. Maybe one of them had, like, a fit of jealousy, and went crazy? Or maybe Ira did it, for the same reason?"

"Ryan *was* kind of an operator. I watched him go around, pulling his crap on all the women. Disgusting."

"I bet *you* didn't let him get away with it."

"That's right, I didn't! Hey, here's a place. This look good to you?" They had reached the brightly it Café de la Place, in the center of Castillac, looking quite inviting in the gray afternoon.

Pascal greeted them at the door. "Bonjour!" he said, and then continued in English, "You would like to sit near the fire?" and gestured to a table by a small hearth at the end of the room where a couple of logs burned.

Patty nodded in an exaggerated way, which was her main method of communicating in France. She and Nathaniel sat at a table by a window where they could feel the warmth of the fire.

"Good-looking waiter, huh?" said Nathaniel, seeing Patty look at Pascal with undisguised admiration.

"You could say that," she admitted, her voice up high.

"So, tell me about your life back home, Patty," he said, smiling. "I know you work as a vet technician, is that right?"

"Yup," she answered, eyes glued to Pascal. "I just really love animals. So that's what I do all day...take care of dogs and cats. My vet is a small-animal vet; she doesn't do horses or anything."

"You ever thought of going to vet school?"

"Not smart enough," said Patty matter-of-factly, though it was not true.

"Welcome to Castillac," said Pascal, arriving at their table with pad at the ready. "You are guests of Molly Sutton, yes?"

"How did you know that?" asked Patty, her expression glowing.

"Ah, I am a detective too, though no match for Molly," Pascal said, laughing, his straight white teeth on display. "I have not seen you before this day. It is not a season of tourists, and there is not much to see here in Castillac anyway. Therefore," he said, drumming his hands on the table in a suspenseful beat, "I guess you are guests of Madame Sutton. 'Guess' and 'guest'...English is not easy," he said, smiling at Patty. "I very much hope you will make this a long stay."

Nathaniel watched Patty practically melt into a puddle of bliss at the attention of the handsome server.

"Molly's place is packed with people this week, and it's been super fun. I just met Nathaniel here a few days ago. And I bet you've heard all about the murder?" chirped Patty.

"I did," said Pascal solemnly. "I am so sorry this has happened during your sojourn. You must understand that France is not full of murdering peoples!"

"Nobody seems to think the killer is from around here," said Nathaniel. "Chief Maron sounds pretty sure it's one of the guests at Molly's. Sort of feels like we're living a TV mystery episode or something!" He made some spooky musical sounds and waved his hands around, but Pascal and Patty were not looking at Nathaniel but each other.

"Your English is *amazing,*" murmured Patty.

Nathaniel raised his eyebrows at her transformation from a skeptical, gossipy woman to a starry-eyed teenage girl.

"Listen, can you tell me where the ladies' room is?" she said to Pascal. "Nathaniel, just order me whatever you're having."

Pascal pointed out the direction of the bathroom, and then turned back to Nathaniel. "What can I get you? Your friend...she is very attractive," said Pascal with a sly grin.

"Yeah, Patty's great. Uh, two coffees, I guess. And do you have cookies, or pastry or something? Bring a plate of that too, please."

"May I ask how long you both plan to stay?"

Nathaniel shrugged. "We've been asked to stay longer, though they can't force us to. I'll probably have to leave at the end of next week—my boss won't let me stay in France indefinitely. Hopefully Chief Maron will wrap things up by then, or least be okay with letting us go."

"And...your friend?" Pascal did not attempt to sound nonchalant about his interest in her, but seemed to be holding his breath, waiting to hear Nathaniel's answer.

Nathaniel stared. "You mean Patty? No idea what she's doing. I haven't heard her say anything about her plans. But," he added, leaning toward Pascal and lowering his voice, "no doubt she needs to get back soon to continue with the treatments. We're all just grateful that she had this one last trip."

Pascal's eyes were wide. "What do you mean?" he whispered.

"Cancer," said Nathaniel, shaking his head sadly. "But please don't say anything. She doesn't like to talk about it, understandably."

"Oh yes," said Pascal. "I'm...so sorry to hear about this. I will bring your coffee right away." Nimbly he moved through the tables on his way to the kitchen, his gorgeous face sorrowful.

❧

WHEN PATTY and Nathaniel returned to La Baraque, Patty thanked him for going to the café with her, and then went to the pigeonnier to check on Ashley.

Nathaniel stood in the yard, trying to decide what to do next. With sudden certainty, he strode to the front door and knocked hard on the French doors. He stood for a moment listening, and heard nothing.

He knocked again, and heard shuffling footsteps.

"Yes?" said Molly, opening the door, not sounding like herself.

"I don't mean to intrude, I hope I'm not bothering you. I'll just say—I'm afraid Constance has blabbed to the rest of us that you're not feeling well. I've had friends get sick with Lyme, and it can be such a bear to recover from! Anyway, the last thing I wanted to do was get you out of bed. Go back and I'll bring you something to drink. I'm sure your doctor has told you to keep hydrated."

"Oh, you're very sweet," said Molly, heading back to her room. "I am thirsty, actually, so thank you."

In a moment Nathaniel came into her room with a glass of ice water. "No bother at all. I know one friend said that the Lyme treatment made everything taste bad to her—is that happening with you, too?"

"Yes! It's the weirdest thing. Even water tastes nasty. No, no, I'm glad you brought me the water and I should be drinking a lot of it. But the taste makes me want to throw up."

"Would you like something other than water to drink?"

"Somehow I don't think Dr. Vernay would be all that keen on my having a kir. And to be honest, it doesn't sound very appetizing, which is really saying something. There might be some juice in the pantry somewhere? Check the floor, behind the bag of rice."

Nathaniel disappeared, then quickly returned with a tall glass of iced apricot juice.

"Oh, right, now I remember! I bought a bottle of that a while ago for some recipe I never ended up making." She took a tiny sip, then gulped some of it down. "That is good! Thank you so much, Nathaniel." She put the glass on her bedside table and fell back on the pillows, exhausted from that small effort. "I'm sorry. I don't know why I'm apologizing, but there it is. I hate this."

He nodded. "Anybody would. You're so fun and energetic, it must be so frustrating and upsetting to be stuck in bed. Has the doctor said when you can expect to feel better?"

Molly shrugged. "He says it depends on a lot of things. Listen, let's not talk anymore about sickness. You're just back from the village? What were you up to?"

"Patty and I went to that café in the center of the village and had some coffee. It's a nice walk and I'm really glad I decided to stay in your gîte instead of getting a hotel room, so I have a chance to make friends. And I do worry a little about women traveling alone. The waiter was making eyes at Patty so I got her out of there and home safe."

"What...Pascal? Oh, I'm sure it was harmless, whatever it was. Listen, would you mind distracting me with something happy? Tell me about Miranda. How did you meet?"

Nathaniel grinned. "Well, it was an unusual meeting, for sure. You know I work in a hospital? Doing computer stuff, not direct health care or anything, so I don't have any contact with patients. But there was this one woman who had been transferred from a hospital in another state, and we were having a devil of a time getting her records to show up in our database. Finally I went to see her myself, wondering whether I could get some kind of idea from her about what was holding things up, thinking maybe the staff had bungled up the information somehow. Anyway, I walked into her room, which was filled with flowers from her friends and family, and there was this incredibly beautiful woman...."

"Oh my! Why was she in the hospital? Is she okay now?"

"Oh yes, absolutely. She had cancer, but a very rare type that her first hospital wasn't qualified to treat. Once she came to us, they got it taken care of and she recovered nicely."

"With plenty of visits from you?" said Molly, smiling, remembering the sweet letter she had read while snooping in his room.

Nathaniel blushed, which Molly found charming. "It's a little weird, or maybe not at all, but my mother had cancer when I was a kid. She died when I was eight years old. So, I don't know, there's a kind of...understanding, maybe? About people who are ill, that I learned during that time."

"I'm so sorry you lost your mother," said Molly, her eyes getting moist.

"Thank you. But really—it was a lifetime ago, and no longer painful. I only brought it up because, well, falling in love with a patient in a hospital might seem unusual."

"Ever read Hemingway's *A Farewell to Arms*? A nurse and a patient. Though I can't think of any cases where the woman is a patient and the doctor falls for her. It's usually the other way around. Anyway, I'm happy for you. I guess we never know where we'll find love, huh?" She took another sip of her juice. "You've been in touch since getting here? What does she think about how crazy this trip has turned out to be?"

"Just emailing mostly, with a couple of real letters and postcards. I…I haven't told anyone about this, because, well, we've only been seeing each other for about two months. But before I left, I asked her to marry me, and she said yes." Nathaniel looked at Molly with shining eyes. "So we're not talking on the phone while I'm over here. We've got a wedding to save up for."

"Well, that is entirely wonderful," said Molly. "Congratulations! Sometimes you just know when something is right," she said, inwardly wondering why that never seemed to happen to her.

"Exactly," agreed Nathaniel.

Molly's face was pale and her freckles stood out even more than usual. She closed her eyes for a moment and sighed deeply. "Thanks, Nathaniel. I think I'm going to try to nap a little now."

"Sure thing, Molly. You need anything, just call."

Molly's thoughts were scattered as she drifted off to sleep for the third time that day. She only hoped this phase of treatment passed quickly so that she could get back to living her life and actively join Ben on the murder case. And where *was* Ben, anyway? Wasn't he going to move in to La Baraque? She couldn't remember whether that conversation had taken place yesterday or last week.

The last thing she wanted to do was be stuck in bed. And with that thought, she began to snore.

23

1987

The curtains were pulled across the window so that everything was dim and gray except for one sharp slit of sunshine that broke across the bed where a woman lay, inexorably moving closer and closer to her face as the sun moved across the afternoon sky.

"Nathaniel," her soft voice said. "Draw the curtains, if you please."

The boy got up and went to the window. He did not look out to the sunny day with yearning, even though he had stayed inside on so many afternoons and missed untold numbers of games with the neighborhood children. He decided himself not to go out, because he was sure that if he did, if he relaxed his vigilance even for one afternoon, one hour—his mother would die.

With some difficulty he managed to get both sections of curtain pulled to the center, and the slice of sun disappeared.

"Thank you, Nathaniel. Come here," his mother said, reaching out her hand. He sat down next to her, arranging his expression as though he were looking at something happy instead of the wasted face of his mother, now down below a hundred pounds, her body ravaged by illness. She said nothing but took his hand in both of hers and held it, closing her eyes. She did this every day. Sometimes Nathaniel waited a half hour or more before she fell asleep or changed position and let go of his hand.

He never let go. Never took himself away from her.

Of course, he was made to go to school every day. His father was in charge of that, and since his mother's illness had been going on for many months, he had gotten used to it in a way, and no longer cried when he was told it was time to leave. He was only eight, so to him, those months were a large chunk of lifetime. In bed at night, when it was time to sleep, he tried to remember how things were before she got sick. He was surprised at how few memories he could grab hold of.

During the work week, Mr. Beech came home every day promptly at seven. He made hamburgers and canned corn for him and Nathaniel to eat, he would tell his son sternly to drink his milk and pick up his shoes from the living room floor, and to do his homework properly. A long list of orders, but never any conversation. Never asked Nathaniel what kinds of books he liked, or whether he was tired of canned corn. Never said how hard it was for all of them, watching his mother drift deeper into illness toward death.

Never laughed, or hugged his son, or managed to see beyond his own sorrow, even for a moment.

24

The next morning, Tuesday, Molly felt quite a bit more human. Tentatively, she got up and got dressed, made coffee, fed Bobo. All of which was more activity than she was used to these last days, yet it didn't feel like too much.

"Bonjour Molls," said Constance, coming in through the front door holding a large pot.

"Bonjour, Constance. Thanks so much for looking after things the way you have been doing. What in the world is that?"

"I just found it sitting on the stoop on my way in. Looks like it's from Monsieur Nugent."

Molly unfolded a note and recognized Edmond Nugent's careful handwriting. He was the owner and sole baker at her favorite place in all of France—Pâtisserie Bujold—and he must have wondered where in the world his most avid customer had disappeared to.

Dearest Molly,

I hear you are not as well as you might be.
Please drink as much soup as you are able.
No matter what is the matter, it will help.

With deepest affection,
Edmond

Molly lifted the lid and peered in. The alluring smell of chicken broth filled her nostrils. "You know, I think I'll have a bowl right now. Want some?" Molly asked Constance.

Before she could answer, a quick rap on the door. Molly went to answer it and found Maron standing outside. "Bonjour Molly. Glad you see you up and about. Lyme treatment not so bad after all?"

"Not at the moment," she said. "What's happening? And where is Ben?"

"I'll explain," he said. "Can I come in?"

"Oh, of course, sorry. Would you like some coffee? Or soup?"

"Coffee, thank you."

Constance had slipped away once she saw who it was. Molly and Maron sat in front of the woodstove and sipped their coffee.

"Ben has been doing a few things for me, sort of under the table. He'll be here shortly."

"Under the table?"

"I mean unofficially. Do you know that Paul-Henri can't stop talking about putting you on the suspect list for Ryan's murder? Or Dedalus, as you've named him."

Molly laughed. "I guess it isn't funny. What did I do to give him such a bad opinion of me?"

"Oh, I don't think he actually believes you did it. It's just that he is such a stickler for form. In his mind, anyone who had contact with Dedalus in the few days he was in Castillac should be on that list. When I asked why the owner of a gîte business would suddenly want to kill one of her guests that she'd never met, he suggested you might have a history with him and lured him over to France to stay in a luxury room so that you could strangle him at your leisure."

"Ah, sort of the Black Widow Innkeeper?" said Molly.

"Precisely," said Maron, with a rare smile. "I would rather know Dedalus's identity before saying anything to the guests, but it's not a perfect world, you know? I can't just sit here and do nothing while the Americans work on that. I don't know whether they are dragging their feet or incompetent, but I am anxious for some progress."

"It's only been a few days."

"Nevertheless. I want to call them in here in a few minutes and tell them about Ryan not actually being Ryan, and I would like you to be here, too, watching and listening. All of them will act surprised, of course. Four will be legitimately shocked, and one will be acting. I'm hoping that between you, me, and Ben, we might be able to spot which one.

"Not Paul-Henri?"

"Unfortunately, Madame Vargas's dog has gotten loose again, so he is otherwise engaged."

"Yves! I love that dog."

"Yes. Well. Can you round the guests up? As I say, I expect Ben at any minute, and I don't mind having everyone get in here ahead of time, wondering what's going on but having to wait to find out. Any added pressure should be helpful to us. You are well enough for this undertaking?"

Molly nodded. "Sure. Before I do that, though, something I've been meaning to tell you." Her face turned a light shade of pink when she confessed to snooping in her guests' quarters. "...so of course once I saw it, I read the letter. It was to his girlfriend back home. Two interesting things about it: he says he's 'pretty sure' the motive was romantic jealousy, which fits with one of our theories; and that he think he knows who did it, but hasn't said anything yet."

"Hmm. You didn't happen to take the letter? Or take a picture of it?"

"Damn. I didn't take it, for obvious reasons, but I had my phone with me and could've snapped a photo. Just didn't occur to me. It was a few days ago now, the letter's probably long since mailed."

"A shame."

"Yes. Well, possibly you can put some pressure on Nathaniel to see who he suspects and why, and at least we can cross him off our own list."

"Don't be too quick about that, Molly."

"It's crystal clear in the letter that he did not do it, Gilles."

"Well, what do you expect him to say to his girlfriend? 'The deed is done and I'll see you soon'? Not likely. You're always the first one to say we should never assume, Molly."

"But..." she started to argue but did not feel up to it. She would fight that battle another day. "Okay then, we can talk more about it later if you're willing. I'll go knock on some doors and be right back. I'm not positive everyone's still around, but it's pretty early..."

While Molly was gone, Maron stood and walked around the living room. He avoided the orange cat, who had taken a chunk out of his calf on a visit back in the summer. He glanced at the books on her bookshelf, opened a drawer, noted the antique glass medicine bottles lined up on the sill of the kitchen window.

Ashley arrived first. "Why bonjour, Offi-si-ay," she said, laying on an accent she had gotten from movies, but not French ones. "I want to tell you, since we're alone? That I'm really so glad you are in charge." She looked at him from under heavily mascaraed eyelashes. "I hope I can be your best witness."

Maron had no idea what to make of this. "Yes. Well, if you can give me any helpful information, I will be glad to hear it. Has anything occurred to you after our last meeting, anything you remembered or forgot to tell me?"

"Well, I'm sure you know that Darcy Bilson had her sights on Ryan? Oh yes. She told Patty—Patty's my college friend, we're traveling together—she told Patty that she wanted Ryan. I mean like, *carnally* wanted him. A married woman, saying something like that to a total stranger! I'm not saying she's guilty, Offi-si-ay Maron, but I do know that when some people don't get what they want, they can go a little cray-cray. Or a *lot.*"

"You are implying that in your opinion, the murderer of Ryan is Darcy Bilson?"

"Yes sir, I am. Or I would be if I were a betting woman, which I am not—because Mama always told me betting is vulgar, and my mama was right about pretty much everything." Ashley snickered to herself at that one, since she had run away from home when she was sixteen in large part to get away from her mother.

Patty came in next, followed in short order by the others.

"We're in luck, Gilles," said Molly. "All present and accounted for. Thanks everyone, I know this is the strangest vacation you've ever had. I will tell you that the gendarmerie of Castillac has distinguished itself over and over during my time here, and hopefully they will soon be able to make an arrest and put this whole thing behind us. I know you're anxious to get home."

"Not really!" blurted Patty. "I mean, I miss my job and all, but you know this is the first time I've ever been in a foreign country, and it's way cool. Plus I could eat those almond croissants all day long."

"Girl after my heart," said Molly. Her mind was feeling clearer than it had in days, and she noticed that Patty, at least, seemed remarkably complacent. Either she was a stone sociopath incapable of feeling guilt, or she was innocent, and knew nothing about what had happened.

"Please make yourselves comfortable," said Maron. "I have some news about the case that you all deserve to know. Ryan Tuck—the man you knew as 'Ryan Tuck'—was an imposter. At this juncture, we do not know his true identity. There does exist a Ryan Tuck, and the passport is valid—but that man is currently in Cincinnati, Ohio, and has never visited France in his life."

Molly observed carefully. All five were motionless, with eyes widened, frozen for a few moments. She couldn't help wondering if Maron was wrong, and the murderer was someone with no connection to La Baraque. Then everyone started talking at once.

"No way!"

"What?"

"I knew there was something fishy about him," said Ira.

"Smooth operator," said Patty.

Darcy and Nathaniel had stood up, mouths open and eyes wide with surprise.

"Then who was he?" asked Darcy.

"As I said," Maron continued, "we do not yet know. But perhaps one of you does?"

Ashley looked down at the floor, her hands fidgeting in her lap. Patty watched her with curiosity, as did Ira.

"Anyone?" asked Maron.

"So what this means is...we don't know if the murderer meant to kill Ryan, or this other guy," said Ira.

Maron nodded.

"Maybe...excuse me if this is not legal or something, but maybe I could help with this? I'm an IT guy, remember. Maybe I could do a search and see what I could come up with?"

"I'm sure the cops have their own IT guys, Nathaniel," said Ashley.

He shrugged, "Yeah, right, sorry Chief, I didn't mean any insult. Just trying to help."

"Thank you for the offer," said Maron. "Molly, could you serve the guests anything to eat and drink? Maybe some coffee at least?"

"Sure!" said Molly, understanding that Maron wanted to keep them in the room. She went to get her tablet, looking up an easy recipe for *sablés* that she'd made before, and got busy in the kitchen.

"You need any help?" Ashley asked her. "I'm no whiz in the kitchen, but honest to God, I'm going to lose my mind if I just stand around out there. I cannot block out of my mind the fact that one of those people is a murderer, like some people seem to be able to."

"Nor should you," said Molly quietly, pretending to assume that of course Ashley herself was above suspicion. She got out the flour, butter, and sugar, and gave Ashley a measuring cup and told her how much sugar to measure out, reminding herself that she was not allowed to eat any cookies while on antibiotics. "So Ashley," Molly continued in a low voice, "just curious—who do you think did it?"

Ashley stopped what she was doing and looked at Molly with wet eyes. "I just...."

Molly held her breath.

But Ashley broke eye contact and went back to measuring out the sugar. "I just miss him, is all. Ryan and I really connected, as I'm sure you noticed. And to have him snatched away like that—"

"I understand. I had affection for him too. Okay, here's the butter. Take the back of this wooden spoon and cream it all together." Molly looked out to the living room. Ira was standing in front of the woodstove, as he liked to do, his arms folded across his wide chest, watching his wife and glancing over at Ashley. Darcy was pacing, her hands in her hair and eyes on the floor. Nathaniel and Patty were sitting next to each other on the sofa, talking in low voices.

Had one of these people really murdered Dedalus? Molly still couldn't quite wrap her head around it. She knew very well that cases are solved with evidence and logical thinking, not emotions and vague impressions. Nevertheless, it did not *feel* to her as though she were in the room with a cold-blooded killer, and it was difficult to shake that feeling off.

Once again, her gaze traveled around the room, watching each guest in turn, wondering what was underneath the public masks they wore. She poured herself another glass of apricot juice and prepared to mingle, ready to eavesdrop, her senses as finely tuned as she could make them.

25

Early Wednesday morning, Patty managed to hustle Ashley out of bed and into a rental car. The drive to Rocamadour would to take a while, and she wanted to be first in line at the Ecopark to see the show that featured falcons and hawks flying free over the valley.

Ashley sat slumped in the passenger seat, sunglasses on. "Are we allowed any breakfast?" she asked crossly. "Or is this forced march not stopping for anything all day?"

"Very funny," said Patty. "Listen, I agreed to come to Castillac only because you promised we could visit this Ecopark thing. Otherwise I would never have wanted to spend my very first trip outside the country coming to a small village where nothing ever happens."

"I would hardly call this trip uneventful."

"Well, okay, but now what? We're holed up at La Baraque with the same people, one of whom might very well be a killer, with nothing to do. I thought the point of traveling was to get out in the world and see stuff?! But all I've done here is walk into the boring village and have coffee."

"Speaking of that, what about that Nathaniel? He's sorta cute, don't you think? Any sparks between you?"

"Nah. Not my type. Plus he has a serious girlfriend. But," Patty said, tightening her grip on the steering wheel and breaking into a grin, "I did meet someone. A server at the Café de la Place. Don't get any ideas about going there, Ash! Seriously! It's *my* territory for the next few days, you hear me?"

"Good Lord, Patty, do you think I just run around trying to steal men away from my friends?"

Patty shrugged. "His name's Pascal. And he is so gorgeous I could hardly breathe."

"Um hm. And you think you have a chance with him? You don't even speak any frawn-say."

"Who cares? His English is magnificent. I don't know, maybe it was just French charm? But he actually seemed interested," Patty said. "At least at first. No tips allowed at the café so I don't think he was just trying to work me for an extra centime. But...."

Ashley waited. "But what?"

"I don't know. He went from warm and interested to sort of avoiding me. It was a little weird. When I went over to thank him and say goodbye, he looked at me all sad. Like he'd lost his best friend."

"So maybe he got some bad news. Everything's not always about you, you know."

"Really?" Patty said sarcastically. "I thought everything was actually all about you."

"I think I should go check this Pascal out. If he's as good-looking as you say, I'd hate for him to be going to waste in a place like Castillac."

"Ash!"

"You just said he was avoiding you. Why shouldn't I have a crack at him? Maybe he likes blondes."

Patty gritted her teeth and said nothing, but her ears turned bright red and she squinted at the road with a dark expression.

The two friends were quiet. They were on an autoroute, and the driving was easy, and before long they were accelerating up a long hill to the parking lot at the very top, where the Ecopark was located. They parked and paid for tickets.

"Aren't birds sort of filthy?" said Ashley. "I mean, they can be pretty and all, but don't a lot of them carry diseases and whatnot?"

"Why do you talk when you have no idea what you're talking about? You sound like a complete airhead."

"Good thing I have other attributes," said Ashley, fluffing up her hair and striking a pose.

Patty rolled her eyes. "Come on, I want to get good seats."

But for the Ecopark show, there were no bad seats. On a bluff overlooking the valley, a few rows of seats ringed an open area, with the drop-off on one side. Handlers came in with gigantic raptors on their arms, and with whistles and treats thrown into the air, the show began. Enormous eagles flew out, wafting on air currents. Falcons dive-bombed for prey and returned to the padded forearms of their handlers. A man came around with a vulture and let it climb on members of the audience if they agreed to it.

"Oh my God," breathed Patty, as the vulture stood on her head. "This is *so* cool!"

Ashley did not hide her distaste. "Is this going on much longer? I am so ready for lunch it's not even funny. And I would like to see the church that's hanging onto the side of the cliff down there."

"Thank you," said Patty to the man with the vulture, who nodded and winked at her. "Raptors are the best."

"I thought you were all about puppies and kittens? Since when did you get interested in a bunch of smelly, flying killing machines?"

"They are not smelly. And just because I work with dogs and cats in my job, doesn't mean I don't appreciate other animals. I love *all* animals, Ashley. A lot more than some people," she added under her breath.

When the show was over, they headed down the path to the tiny village, which clung to the side of a high cliff. It was breathtaking, and impossible not to wonder at the work that had made the place possible. How had they managed the engineering, or even getting the materials up so high? The accomplishment was not simply having constructed buildings in that most unimaginable location, it was that the buildings were so beautiful. Luminous in the sunshine, delicate and yet powerful.

Patty and Ashley wandered the narrow streets, bought postcards and ice cream, and eventually got to the church. Patty walked through quickly, hoping to have time for another quick visit to the Ecopark on their way out, but Ashley lit candles. Then she entered a pew, knelt on a dusty velvet kneeler and closed her eyes to pray.

Patty watched her. It occurred to her for the first time that her friend was sort of the human embodiment of a raptor: always hungry, always ready to snatch away anything it wanted from anyone.

Eventually Ashley got up and they made their way up the long stairs to the parking lot. It was already getting dark and the Ecopark was closing. Near the top was a landing where you could stop to catch your breath and admire the view, and Ashley, panting hard, went to the edge and leaned her hands on the low railing.

Patty stood behind her. She took in her friend's gold sandals, the worst possible shoes for all the walking they had planned to do. She took in her teased hair, her habit of always posing, as though the world was always clamoring with cameras to capture everything she did. She thought of Pascal and his dazzling smile.

She came up behind her old friend, and put both palms on her back. Given Ashley's position, she realized it would be easy to push her. So easy. And so, so satisfying.

26

1990

Patty had a plan. She was thrilled to have gotten her first invitation to a party with the popular kids in her class at Jackson Middle School, but there was no way on God's green earth that her mother would allow her to go. It was not even worth asking. What Patty needed was a distraction, something to send her mother into a tizzy long enough for Patty to get away unnoticed.

Which is where her little brother Dwayne came in.

Dwayne, bless his heart, was not as clever as Patty—no one in the family was, to be sure—and she often used him for her own ends. He was sent to the store for candy they weren't supposed to eat, cards they weren't supposed to play, magazines they weren't supposed to read. When the contraband was discovered (which it almost always was), it was Dwayne who suffered, because Patty had convinced him that there was no point in both of them being punished. So he was spanked and not allowed to watch cartoons and even shunned at the dinner table, and while he protested the injustice to Patty, he never tattled on her.

In her religious fervor, Mrs. McMahon believed that almost anything fun was the work of the devil, hence much of what an eighth-grader wanted to do was not allowed. No rock music, no unapproved television shows, no dancing, certainly no unsupervised fraternizing with boys...and what Patty McMahon wanted to do, with every fiber of her being, was fraternize with Bobby Selden, somewhere—anywhere—that was private.

"Look," she whispered to Dwayne. "Just take the radio out of the garage and up to the attic. There's a plug up there, I checked. No one's going to hear it all the way up there."

"If she does hear it, I'm dead."

"She won't! Plus the attic stairs are steep and narrow. If you hear her coming, just turn it off and shove it into one of those old trunks. By the time she gets up there, you can be lounging around, reading a comic book."

"But that'll get me in trouble! You know she hates comics."

"Right, Dwayne," said Patty, slowly. "That's the whole idea. Give her something little to get mad about, and she'll forget the bigger thing. See? She'll shout about the comic but probably won't even punish you. But the radio, hoo boy."

"I know. She'd never let me leave the house again."

"Yep. So don't get caught. You're smarter than she is, Dwayne!"

"You think so?" he asked hopefully.

"You betcha."

The plan did work, after a fashion. Mrs. McMahon was screaming in the attic long enough to give Patty time to slip away with her knapsack full of borrowed, not-allowed clothing. She ran to the bus stop and rode into town, changing in the bathroom in the drugstore, and made it to the party with the popular kids.

As punishment, Dwayne had to spend two hours praying when he got home from school every day for a week, and wouldn't talk to Patty for days. But she didn't care. The party had been a big disappointment, and she had moved on to her next goal: get through high school with a high enough grade point average to get a scholarship to Auburn. Anything to get away from home.

27

"I'm so glad you're feeling better. You look amazing, you know that?" Ben took Molly's hand as they started down the path in the woods that branched off from the meadow at La Baraque.

"Flatterer. Keep talking."

"And you really do feel better? You're not just pretending, to keep people from nursing you to death?"

"Constance has been driving me crazy. At least now I know it's not true that everyone in France is a good cook."

"I thought Lawrence was in charge of food. Have you been starving while I was away?"

"Lawrence has arranged to have meals dropped off almost every day. But he's got some business thing going on up in Brittany, so he's been in and out of town. Honestly, everything feels so fragmented, with Franny and Nico still gone too. And you! Where have you disappeared to lately?"

"I hope you're not feeling neglected. I've missed you."

"I manage just fine," Molly said, with a slight edge of defensiveness that made her wince. "But come on, tell me."

"Maron's been hitting some roadblocks with the embassy. You understand how it is—no one knows him there, so it's understandable they're nervous about an American getting murdered here, and the potential diplomatic fallout from that. Anyway, I know some people in Paris, some people in law enforcement, so I went up to meet with them in person. These days you have to be careful what you write in email or say over the phone, which meant my friends all wanted to talk in cafés or out walking, where it's safer."

"Jeez, you've gone all cloak and dagger on me!"

Ben laughed, and the sound made all the tension in Molly's body drain away. "Hardly," he said. "But they told me that Dedalus's identity has been confirmed. He was a man named Jim Pyke, American, from Maryland."

"Not Ohio, where Ryan Tuck is from?"

"No."

"But they must have known each other, right? How else would Pyke...or I don't know, maybe another person's identity is something you can buy online these days, just like shoes?"

"You know about the dark web?"

"No. Is that like a black market?"

"Precisely. An online black market. And you can get pretty much anything you want on it, just like in the old-fashioned, in-person kind."

They walked along, thinking this over.

"So did you find anything out about this Jim Pyke? Anything to link him to anybody we know?"

"Not so far."

"How did they figure out his identity? It's still so hard for me to grasp that the man I got to know—the man who threw sticks for Bobo!—was someone else altogether. I'm guessing he had a record?"

"Yes. Pyke was an embezzler, and not a very good one. He'd been gotten caught multiple times and served time twice. We're lucky on that score, that he'd been in the American prison system—it meant they had fingerprints. Recently he had managed to get a job at a non-profit, some sort of education venture for poor children. Apparently Pyke bled it dry and then skipped town, after arranging first to impersonate Ryan Tuck, of course. No connection between the two men as far as anyone can tell, except neither one was anyone you'd want to be pals with."

"Was it Nathaniel who said that Ryan—I mean Dedalus...wait, *Pyke*, Jim Pyke. I'm having the hardest time keeping the names straight! Remember, Pyke told Patty that he had done something wrong, something he was in trouble for."

"Embezzling from a non-profit would fit, certainly."

Molly nodded. "It's weird. If you'd given me a list of qualities and asked me to check off which ones I thought Pyke had, I'd have checked 'generosity' without hesitation. Guess I had him all wrong."

Wisely, Ben did not comment, but put his arm around Molly's shoulders and pulled her closer. The woods weren't showing any sign of spring yet and the sky was gray.

"It's just around the next curve," said Molly quietly.

"Where you found him?"

"Yup."

They walked quickly to the spot. The area still looked disturbed: leaves were trampled, and a few small branches had broken off and lay on the ground.

"Which tree?" asked Ben, and Molly pointed.

"It would be easy to climb, with those thick lower branches," she said. "I guess, after Pyke was strangled, the killer slipped the noose over his head, tossed the rope up over the branch, and yanked him up until his feet were off the ground."

"And what did Nagrand say when he got here? Did he think Pyke had put the noose on himself, and then jumped off the branch?"

"I can't say. The place was crawling with the forensics team and Maron was here. I couldn't really ask a ton of questions without making a nuisance of myself."

Ben nodded slowly. "Thanks for showing me the site. I can only hope that the discovery of the real victim helps move the case forward, because otherwise? We are knee-deep in mud."

Molly dropped onto a log rather suddenly, trying and failing to push her hair out of her face.

"You okay?"

"No. I mean yes. Overall. I just forget that I have to take it sort of easy. Fatigue sneaks up on me and boom! I just want to be in bed, even though I felt okay two seconds ago."

"That's easy to fix," he said, scooping her into his arms. She let her head fall against his broad chest and couldn't help smiling as he trotted down the path toward home.

❧

BEN GOT MOLLY TUCKED into bed with her tablet and a tall glass of apricot juice, and then went upstairs to his room to make a few calls, thinking that he really needed to spend more time around La Baraque. She was still fragile, and of course there was the matter of one of the guests being a potential danger. Though it was always possible that Paul-Henri's mystery man was responsible for the murder after all.

He is such a thoroughly decent man, Molly was thinking as she opened a novel but did not start to read it. She felt so tired, and her thoughts pinged around her head, all helter-skelter again. Dr. Vernay had told her to expect this pattern of feeling worse just after taking the medication, then gradually a bit better, then drifting down again before the next dose was due. Over time, he had said, the bad phases will be less bad and shorter, and the good phases will get better and longer.

Please be right, Dr. Vernay, she murmured, letting her eyes close.

"Hey Molly?"

Her eyes snapped open. "Oh, hi Nathaniel. Here I am, in bed

again. I guess I overdid it a little. But I hope after a nap I'll be up again and available. Is everything all right?"

"Oh sure! I'm just sticking my head in to see if there's anything you need."

"I don't think so. Well, if you could close those curtains, that would be terrific. My eyes are really sensitive to light at the moment."

Nathaniel crossed the room and busied himself with the curtains while Molly watched. She wanted to ask him about the other guests, but could not find the energy to make the words come out.

"Okay, I'm off. Just give me a call if you need something."

Molly nodded and Nathaniel left, closing the bedroom door quietly behind him.

I wish these guests would give me some peace, she thought. But Nathaniel's a sweet kid. Losing his mother must have been just awful. And then, in a flash (the way good ideas often seem to come), she wondered if she could send Miranda a plane ticket so she could join him at La Baraque, as a way to thank Nathaniel for his kindness. Molly had definitely discovered her inner spendthrift after coming into her riches back in December; the idea of splurging on a plane ticket for a women she'd never met tickled her.

Her laptop was on a small table next to the window. Molly considered getting up and buying the ticket right then, but realized she would need Miranda's last name and probably address and email as well. Her eyelids were getting heavier and heavier. She sat up and sipped the juice, trying to figure out a way to get those details without asking Nathaniel and giving the surprise away, but for the life of her, she couldn't focus, and slowly slipped down under the heavy comforter and once again to sleep.

28

Maron and Monsour took the small police car to La Baraque. Maron had called ahead to ask Molly to gather the guests together once again so that he could announce the true identity of the murder victim.

"It does seem to me that merely observing their faces when we give them the news is not exactly an advanced tool of detection," Paul-Henri said as they bumped over a part of the road that needed repairing. "Can't we simply bring them in and interrogate them?"

"We can bring them in, yes. But we don't want to give them time to organize their thoughts and get their defenses up. I want to see them as a group, see who glances at who, who is startled by the news and who is not. This first reaction may tell us who to focus on. Law enforcement in Paris and in the States are working on finding the connection between Pyke and one of these tourists. It exists and it *will* be found. It's only the lack of time that concerns me. Soon they will head back home, and legally, there's not a thing I can do to stop them."

"Presumably, even if they do return home, that does not mean the murderer goes free, yes? If we find the connection next month, or next year—the perpetrator can be picked up then, I suppose?"

"That's a lot of time to go into hiding and start a new life somewhere else."

"I would think that would be difficult these days, what with face-recognition technology and rampant spying by pretty much everyone."

Maron sighed. "Look, Paul-Henri, just try to stay positive, all right? I understand there are many ways for this investigation to go wrong, but it doesn't do anyone any good to dwell on them. At this meeting I will tell everyone about Pyke. You are to observe carefully. I am especially interested in the reactions of Ira and Darcy Bilson. I don't know if you've heard the gossip, but Darcy apparently blew her top out at Lela Vidal's farm the other day. She's unstable and I want us to keep an eye on her."

"And her husband?"

"Well, he's big enough to have managed the physical difficulties of the murder without any trouble, for starters. And underneath that jolly exterior, I think he is an angry man. Angry at the world, and especially his wife."

"I have seen him behaving quite gently toward her."

"That's called being a doormat, Paul-Henri. Others have reported that Darcy has wild mood swings, like I said, and he works double overtime trying to keep her from going off. Maybe this time, with his wife flirting with another man right under his nose, in front of everyone—maybe *he's* the one who went off."

"Perhaps," said Monsour. "I have not had a chance to tell you: I've been asking around the village about the man Christophe saw on the night of the murder. I have one point of confirmation."

"Someone else saw this person?"

"Yes. Malcolm Barstow."

Maron laughed. "Malcolm! That boy lies like the rest of us breathe. I can promise you this—if Malcolm said he saw a stranger in a dark coat, he's got a self-serving reason for saying so.

Probably wants to have him blamed for something Malcolm has done."

Monsour sniffed and did not answer.

They turned into the driveway of La Baraque and made their way to the front door with Bobo jumping up on Monsour and leaving muddy prints on his trousers.

"Blast it," muttered Monsour, trying to rub off the mud, while Maron suppressed a snicker.

The front door swung open before they had a chance to knock. "Bonjour Gilles, Paul-Henri," said Ben, gesturing for them to come in. "I'm afraid Molly is resting, but I've made sure all the guests are in the living room."

To a person, they looked wary. Nathaniel and Patty sat next to each other on the sofa; Ira stood in front of the woodstove; Darcy waited apart from the group but for once did not go into a headstand. Ashley was curled up in an armchair with a blanket pulled up around her.

"All right then, thank you for coming. I do appreciate your forbearance in this drawn-out matter. And I want you to know that we are doing everything we can to bring the investigation to a rapid conclusion. We have made some progress."

All eyes were glued on the Chief. Ben and Paul-Henri watched the guests carefully.

"The murder victim was a man named James Pyke, known as Jim. He was from Frederick, Maryland, and had not visited France before this trip."

"Looks like he picked the wrong place for a vacation," muttered Patty, and Darcy shot her a dark look.

Dressed in a bathrobe and with her hair a fright, Molly appeared and slipped into the kitchen to make herself a cup of green tea. Feeling a bit better after the nap, she went into the pantry to look for the tea without anyone noticing her presence.

"So, does anyone know or have any connection to Jim Pyke?" Maron asked, but he could see from their closed-up expressions he would get nothing. The tourists shrugged or shook their heads. Ashley sat frozen, an artificial smile on her heavily made-up face. Patty and Nathaniel talked quietly about going to the Café de la Place again as soon as Maron let them go. The Bilsons drifted to the edge of the living room, as far from Maron as they could get without leaving altogether, and talked in low voices.

"I told you," said Ira.

"Okay, okay, you were right and I was wrong. Happy now?"

"You gonna tell him?"

"What good would that do? They already know who it is now."

Molly stood in the pantry listening. She listened hard, leaning toward the opening of the pantry door but not risking taking a step and being heard. So if she was interpreting that correctly, the Bilsons knew who Jim Pyke was. Why had they not said anything? How exactly did they know him? And what did it mean?

29

The mood at La Baraque had been understandably strange ever since Pyke's murder. By turns giddy, frightened, and bored, that Thursday night the guests made one last effort to enjoy themselves and return to the happy few days of socializing they had experienced on first arriving. The Valentine's Day party was back on—days past February 14th, but nonetheless anticipated eagerly, at least by Ira whose idea it was.

Not wanting to bother Molly, Ira had asked Constance and Ben for help with food. Constance, knowing her limitations, had brought a few dishes from the traiteur: a Périgord walnut tart that would remind Ashley of the Southern staple, pecan pie, and a small bag of prunes stuffed with foie gras. Ben had set up a grill behind the house and was cooking duck breasts, rare, slicing them thin so they could soak up a great deal of the peppercorn sauce he had bubbling on the stove.

At one point, Molly came out to the kitchen to see how things were going, saw with approval that Ben was wearing one of her aprons, and crawled back into bed, intending to join the party once it got going.

Ira had driven to Bergerac to get a good deal on some champagne, and Ashley contributed some candles "to make the atmosphere less dreary."

"I feel bad for not lifting a finger to help," Nathaniel said to Ira when everyone was just arriving.

"Eh, here you go," said Ira, handing him a bottle of unopened champagne.

Nathaniel's face turned pink.

"Don't know how? At your age?" Ira shook his head. "Don't worry about it. I sure didn't grow up drinking this stuff either. First, take that metal thing off the top, right, like that. Now put a dishtowel over the cork—here—and slowly twist the bottle. The bottle, not the top. That's it. Get ready—"

The loud pop made Darcy flinch and Ashley come running. "Now that is some music to my ears!" she said, her Southern accent even heavier than usual. "Sill voo play and mair-see!" she laughed, holding out an empty glass to catch some of the foam dribbling from the top.

Patty rolled her eyes. "I don't speak French but even I can tell you: she can't either," she said to Darcy, who nodded and then jostled her way in, holding out a glass.

"Please, everyone must try a prune with foie gras...especially if you've never tasted one," said Constance in French. None of the guests understood the words, but since she held out a plate of nicely arranged prunes and gestured to them, they got the point.

"Liver is gross," said Ashley, as she smiled and nodded at Constance. "I'll eat that over my dead body."

Taking a second one, Darcy flashed a rare smile at Constance and said, "This is probably the most delicious thing I've ever eaten. Except for cheese."

Once everyone had finished a first glass of champagne, the mood of the party perked up considerably. Ben had managed to find an old boom box and was playing French classics that involved plenty of accordions, and he danced Constance around for a few minutes until she was giggling too hard to continue. Patty and Ashley stood by the kitchen counter eating a *cabécou* that Darcy had contributed.

"I just can't help thinking about what my great-great-grandfather would have thought about all this. He was French, you know," said Ashley.

"French-Canadian?"

"No, silly, Paris-French. You know me as Ashley Gander but our name used to be pronounced Gahn-DAY, you know."

Patty started chuckling and a bit of cheese went down the wrong pipe. Coughing, she made her way to the kitchen to get some water, with Ashley following behind. "Well, it seems like no one's even talking about the murder anymore," said Ashley, leaning close to Patty's ear to speak. "I mean, besides the cops. But what about us? Don't our opinions count for anything?"

"Um, no? Why should they?" said Patty, when the coughing was over. "It's not like it gets decided by a vote." Patty sometimes thought Ashley was dumber than a pile of rocks.

"I'm just gonna say," said Ashley, "only between you and me and don't go blabbing, that *I* think the murderer is Nathaniel."

"What? He's the nicest person here!"

"Exactly! He's too nice. You just know those nice ones are the worst trouble of all."

Patty shook her head. "No, I *don't* know that. In fact, he's sitting over there all by himself and I'm going to go talk to him."

"Keep him away from your neck, is all I'm saying."

"Oh, please," said Patty, rolling her eyes dramatically, leaving Ashley in the kitchen. As she walked by, Darcy offered her more cheese.

"Different kind," she said. "It's a *Bleu des Causses*, from the next county over. It'll knock your socks off!"

"Will you just shut up about cheese?" Patty snapped. Ira glanced over, along with Ashley.

"What're you so on edge about, anyway?" asked Darcy.

"Well," said Patty, changing her expression and tasting a bit of cheese on a cracker, "I have to admit, that is some seriously tasty cheese. So listen, I'm curious, and running a little survey. Who do *you* think killed Ryan?"

"You mean Pyke?"

"Right. Yeah—Pyke."

Darcy shrugged and looked at the floor.

"I'm worried it might be Ash," Patty whispered, and Darcy's head started up.

"Why do you say that?"

"She's been off her head ever since we got here. Not herself. And last night, she was talking in her sleep. Kept moaning and saying 'I'm sorry!' Dragging it out like some kind of ghost, you know? 'I'm soooorrrrryyyy.'"

"That's all you got? Just that she's been acting funny and talking in her sleep?"

Nathaniel came over and asked Patty to dance, and she shrugged at Darcy and went to the center of the room and let Nathaniel steer her through a sort of jitterbug. "How'd you learn to dance like this?" she said in his ear, during a slow part.

"My father made me take dancing lessons after my mother died," he said.

"Cool."

"No, not really. He just wanted me out of the house and didn't care how or why. I had tuba lessons too."

Patty guffawed at the image of a baffled young Nathaniel blowing away on a tuba. They went for another glass of champagne. Ashley and Ira danced, Darcy glared and ate more cheese, and the party staggered on, all the gaiety and innocence of their first meetings gone no matter how hard they tried to get them back. Ben lurked about, bringing fresh glasses or replacing a box of crackers as cover for his shameless eavesdropping (though his English was not fully up to the task). Eventually he slipped away to find Molly and see how she was doing.

"Not bad," she said, already up and dressed in blue jeans and a silky top. "Let me just get my hair up into a bun and I'll be right out. Have you heard anything interesting? Anyone behaving badly?"

"It's quite a crew out there," said Ben in his typical dry tone. "For a Valentine's party, there is rather a dearth of love, I would say. None of them seem to like each other much at all."

"I know," said Molly, twisting her hair up and pinning it. "Before the murder, it was one big, happy family. Well, not quite —more like one big, complaining grouchy family. But a family just the same. But come on, give me some specifics. What are they talking about?"

"Eh, cheese, mostly. I've got nothing so far. You're really feeling better? Then come on, let's get the champion eaves-dropper out on the field!"

When Molly entered the room, the guests broke into applause, though their expressions looked more tipsy than actually pleased to see her. Molly made the rounds, talking for a minute or two with each guest, and then sat on the sofa next to Nathaniel.

"I'm sure it's a bit sad to be at a Valentine's party without your valentine," said Molly, sounding more energetic than she felt.

Nathaniel shook his head. "It is, for sure. But I'm having a good time. You missed Patty and me on the dance floor," he added shyly.

"Very sorry to miss that! Maybe you'll do an encore?"

He smiled and nodded, about to tell Molly about all the lessons his father had made him take, but she interrupted to ask about Miranda's last name. "I'm only asking because I've got a friend here in the village who has an antique shop. Well, a junk shop, really, but sometimes he's got some nice stuff. Anyway, there's tons of old monogrammed pieces, anything from silver to plates. And so, I don't know if I'll get around to going anytime soon, but—is Miranda planning to take your name, do you know?

If she is, I might be able to find something with her new monogram on it. A quirky, interesting gift from your trip."

"Aw, Molly, that's really thoughtful of you," he said, looking at her warmly. "Her last name's Cunningham. She's going to take my name—I told her it was fine either way—and so she'll be Miranda Cunningham Beech."

"Very stately," Molly said with a smile. "Okay, if I get around to Lapin's shop, I'll keep my eye out for MCB. No promises, but something might turn up."

"Thanks, Molly. Can I get you a drink, or a plate of something to eat?"

At that moment, Ben arrived at Molly's side with another glass of apricot juice (She was getting really sick of the stuff now).

"Thanks, Nathaniel, I'm good." He nodded and went to find Patty.

"Anything?" Ben whispered. Molly motioned for him to follow and went far enough down the corridor that they could talk without being overheard.

"I realized I forget to tell you something from yesterday. I swear being sick has turned my brain into a slab of Swiss cheese. Anyway, when Maron was here telling the group about Pyke, I overheard the Bilsons talking. It seemed fairly clear that they had already known about Pyke's true identity."

"What did they say?"

"Ira was saying 'I told you so,' and Darcy...something like... there's no point telling them now, they already know who it is."

"Interesting."

"Indeed." Molly continued, "Well, in the absence of any forensic or other evidence coming from Maron or the embassy, here's how it looks. Nathaniel's out because of the letter. Patty's out because she's a tiny little thing, too small to have overcome Pyke even with surprise on her side. That leaves Ashley and the Bilsons. Out of those three, I'm sort of leaning toward Ira. He's big and strong, possibly seething with resentment at being married to someone as difficult as Darcy. He knew that Ryan was actually Pyke but said nothing. Plus—I think I forgot to tell you about this, too—Constance found a needle kit in the cottage."

"A what?"

"I know! I told her it could be for a million things and totally on the level. But Constance was convinced it was for heroin. Said she saw a little baggie of it and everything. I know that being a drug addict doesn't mean he's a murderer, but it does mean he's out of control, you know? It's too bad Maron has not been able to search everyone's rooms."

"I guess he doesn't need to," Ben said drily.

Molly elbowed him. "It *is* my property, after all," she said, and then, sounding worried, "Could I get in trouble? Do you think I broke the law?"

"With your snooping? Eh, Constance was cleaning, wasn't she? And you could make the excuse of checking to make sure everything was in order. Unless you were doing things like ripping out the seams in someone's coat looking for hidden pockets?"

"No seam-ripping has occurred."

Ben kissed the top of her head. "Good. You will dodge an arrest then."

"And how about you? Any ideas about who the killer is?"

"I try not to make assumptions," he answered, teasing her with her own words. "Right now, all five are possible as far as I can tell."

"There's a lot going on under the surface that we don't know about yet."

Ben nodded. "And unfortunately, we're running out of time. I expect they will be heading home in a few days. Maron can't do anything to hold them, and the authorities in Paris and Ohio—and now Maryland—have produced nothing."

"You know what? This case is depressing me. It's bad enough

that I've spent the last week mostly asleep—how are we supposed to solve this thing without any evidence? I'm having a kir."

"Didn't Doctor...." Ben started to say, but then shrugged and went to make it for her.

Darcy and Nathaniel had left. Patty and Ashley were arguing about what to do the next day. Ira, more than a little tipsy, had cornered Constance in the kitchen.

"I've told you about the dairy? We want a big herd of goats, just like Lela Vidal's. We're gonna make the best cheese," he said, taking Constance by the shoulders so that she backed up against the refrigerator. "Award-winning cheese. That milking room will be covered with blue ribbons!" He looked down at the floor, his eyes welling up. Constance considered making a break for it but something about the man provoked pity. "Darlin'," he said in a low voice, "I'm worried. I can tell you that because after we get out of here, I'm never gonna see you again. Plus I don't think you understand English, am I right?"

Constance shrugged, only catching his tone but not the words. He was standing too close and she tried to edge away, but he loomed over her and put his hand against the wall next to her. She took a deep breath and waited for him to finish talking.

"It's my wife," he said, his voice cracking. "I'm worried...I think she might have...you've got to understand, the woman is impulsive. She doesn't mean it, you know? I...."

"Monsieur Bilson!" said Ben, coming into the kitchen. "Have you seen the crème de cassis?"

Ira broke away from Constance and wiped his eyes. "Nope. I've been sticking to champagne all night. When in Rome, is what I always say." He moved around Ben and began collecting dirty dishes and stacking them on the counter.

With a wave goodnight, Constance scurried home to Thomas, leaving only Molly, Ben, and Ira, and a room wrecked by a sullen party.

"Where has everyone gone?" Molly asked. "I hate to see you stuck with all the cleaning up, Ira."

"I don't mind," he said, lumbering around the room with a tray, picking up dirty glasses.

Oh yes you do, thought Molly, but she kept it to herself.

30

The morning after the party, Molly was moving slowly. She settled at her desk with a cup of coffee, anxious to deal with her correspondence. She hadn't checked her email in days and hoped she didn't have a throng of prospective guests who already felt neglected by her silence. There were a number of queries. Methodically, she went through them, answering questions about Castillac and the Dordogne generally, the weather, and the food.

It was such pleasant work, helping people plan their vacations. For the hundredth time, she felt grateful to be able to be there, to have her business and her life in Castillac. Even with the stupid ticks. And if she could only get well enough to start this new venture with Ben, life would be pretty damn near perfect. The thought that so far they were failing utterly on their very first (unofficial) case prickled on the outer edge of her consciousness but for the moment, she successfully pushed it away.

With her mailbox finally empty, she clicked idly around the web, reading articles and blogs on various topics, losing track of time. Just as she was about to go finish cleaning up the kitchen from the night before, she remembered her surprise idea for

Nathaniel: buying a plane ticket for Miranda Cunningham. He had been so kind to her, and the idea of supporting their young love pleased her—as did her newfound ability to spend such a large sum of money more or less on a whim. But it was probably too late for such a gesture, she thought. All the guests, including Nathaniel, would probably be gone by the middle of the week, and it wasn't worth such a long trip for only a few days.

Curious about what Miranda looked like, she typed "Miranda Cunningham" into the search engine, and clicked "enter." The first few entries were strange sorts of hybrids, featuring French text with Anglo names. The following set were ads offering to find the phone number, address, and criminal record of a Miranda Cunningham, for only a small fee.

And then, on the following page, she saw "Miranda Cunningham—Obituary."

Her heart in her throat, Molly clicked and began to read.

31

Miranda had died three months ago of gliosarcoma. She was survived by her mother. No siblings.

Well, it must be a different Miranda Cunningham, Molly thought. She typed 'gliosarcoma' into the search engine, looking for the number of cases per year, but apparently it was so uncommon, researchers struggled to find enough of it to study.

So. Statistically, it would be virtually impossible for two people of the same name to have recently died of the same rare disease. She didn't need to be good at math to see that.

Well. That poor, broken-hearted boy. Nathaniel had so much wanted to believe his beloved was still here, just for a little longer, thought Molly. She was torn between sympathy and the understanding that his fantasy was a few steps past sane. But at the same time, she understood that people sometimes traveled so that they could remake their reality, one way or another. Some pretended to be wilder than they were at home, take more risks, be free of the self everyone knew. And in Nathaniel's case, keep Miranda alive for a few extra days.

Death. Who doesn't want to fight it?

It's so very hard to let go, she thought, while acknowledging that in her own life, she had not really had to face that kind of loss yet. The death of her parents had been difficult, certainly, but their relationship had been tepid, and she had never doubted that, with time, she would get past the grief. It had been sad, and of course she still missed them. But the loss had not been what Nathaniel was facing, the death of his beloved when he was still intoxicated with her.

Molly stood up from the desk and felt a bit lightheaded, so she put her hands on its surface until the feeling passed. She needed to get out of the house, get some fresh air and a change of scene. She texted Lawrence and asked him to meet her at Chez Papa for an early lunch, and he wasted no time answering with an emoji smile.

Within the half hour, the two friends sat on their usual stools grinning at each other.

"I'm so very glad to see your freckled face," said Lawrence. "And terribly sorry to have been absent so much. This thing in Brittany—"

"Don't give it a thought," said Molly. "Believe me, I have had plenty of company. More than enough. And I've loved the food you've been sending. The traiteur really does a great job with the chicken pie, don't they?"

"Yes. I eat it so often, it's a wonder I can fit through the door."

Molly smiled. She was so happy to have the kind of friend where they could not see each other for a while, and pick up right where they left off as though one of them had just gone into another room for a few minutes.

"So tell me, with as much detail as you like: how are you feeling?"

Molly sighed. "Crappy, to be honest. It's up and down. Sometimes I feel almost like my old self, and sometimes I'm just flattened with exhaustion. And my brain doesn't work right."

"You're just old."

"You're so hilarious," said Molly, shooting him a dirty look.

"You know I'm just teasing you. And what about the murder case? Surely that has given you something to live for?"

"Well, yes and no. It's frustrating to feel like I'm napping straight through important stuff. And I'm..." she put her hand on Lawrence's arm, noticing the fine fabric of his sport coat, "I'm just really grateful to have friends like you, people in my life who are solid. I know everyone probably has secrets, or rather episodes from their past they wouldn't want broadcast to the world. But this group staying at La Baraque...it feels like there is so much hidden, you know? Like they're wearing disguises and the rest of us don't really have any idea who they are."

"Are you talking about the stolen identity?"

"Well, that's part of it, for sure. I mean, I really liked the guy who I thought was Ryan but turned out to be Jim. It's shaken me, getting taken in like that. And Ben tells me that he's—Jim, I mean —he was a two-bit embezzler who was in prison twice. Yet there I was, la la la, feeding him gougères and laughing at his jokes and thinking he was just sweet and cute as can be. I let him kiss me, for crying out loud."

Lawrence bit the side of his cheek to stop himself from looking amused. Then he relented. "Look, Molly, how long did you know the man—a day or two? I have absolutely no doubt that if he had managed to live out the week, you would have gotten a clearer idea of his true nature. Or, maybe he was embezzling for reasons other than his own enrichment? Maybe his beloved sister has shocking medical bills and he was trying to raise money to help her."

"You should make movies with an imagination like that. But I appreciate your trying to get me off the hook. Anyway, I just want to make sure you know how much I value your friendship—and the rest of the crew, as well: Nico and Frances, and even Lapin and Nugent. You all might drive me crazy from time to time, but I trust you. I trust all of you with my life."

"And I daresay you cannot say the same about your guests."

Molly shook her head. "No. All right, let's eat! I'm suddenly starving for a plate of *frites*. I don't care what else we have but let's start with that, shall we?" She waved at the bartender, acutely missing Nico, and asked Lawrence to tell her all the news she had missed. "You can start with Lapin's girlfriend."

"Jealous?"

Molly swatted his shoulder and laughed. "Come on, I know you have dirt. Spill!"

32

The workers arrived a few weeks earlier than expected, which for Molly was excellent news. She had her heart set on installing a natural swimming pool at La Baraque, and the December windfall had made it possible. Since the end of winter had been on the mild side, the excavator pulled into the driveway, ready to go.

Molly gave the driver a cup of coffee while they waited for the pool designer to show up. She asked him about other projects he had worked on and how they had turned out, and felt excited that work was finally beginning. At one end of the meadow behind La Baraque was a small spring. Most of the time, it was not big enough to make a stream, more of a soggy spot where your socks might get wet. Hopefully, the designer's judgment that the water source was sufficient would turn out to be correct. Several systems of natural filtration would be put in, along with a solar-powered pump. The bottom was to be covered with a thick rubber mat, and water-loving plants installed all around the edge.

It was hardly swimming weather, but Molly was still giddy at the prospect. The designer finally arrived with another workman, and the job officially got started.

Unfortunately, however, it was a medication day, and once the immediate thrill of seeing the machine's bucket bite into the earth wore off, Molly felt sick to her stomach. Her arm was tingling and she knew she belonged in bed. Damn it to hell, she muttered under her breath, inviting Bobo to come into her bedroom as she changed into flannel pajamas and got back in bed.

She slept, dreaming of blue waterfalls and flowers, and also of a frightening young woman, lying motionless on a bed, her face paler than pale.

Someone was knocking softly. "Who is it?" she said, barely conscious but wanting to escape the dream.

"Hey," said Nathaniel. "Am I bothering you? Sorry, I'll see you later."

"No, no, don't go," said Molly, struggling to sit up and get all the way awake. "There's something I want to talk to you about."

"Anything!" he said with a smile.

Molly gestured for him to sit in the slipper chair by the window. "It's a little awkward," said Molly. "But I found something out I want to share with you, not to accuse you, but I...I want you to know that you don't have to suffer your grief all alone." She wondered if that would be enough to let him know what she was going to say.

He looked curious, and a little guarded.

"I was feeling sorry that you've been stuck here at La Baraque all this time, separated from your fiancée," she said. "People might say being stuck in France is hardly the worst thing, and of course I agree with that. But I also remember what it's like to be young and in love, and...and so, I had this idea of sending Miranda a plane ticket so she could join you."

Nathaniel's cheeks got very pink but he did not say anything.

"And...I'm sorry if this seems like a violation of your privacy, Nathaniel, and please know that my intentions are only good. But in trying to manage this surprise, I ended up finding out that Miranda had passed away."

Nathaniel took a long breath in through his nose. There was a long, uncomfortable silence. "Just say 'died,' Molly. She died."

"Yes. She died. I'm so very sorry."

He buried his face in his hands. "People act as though saying the word *die* is going to bring the Grim Reaper straight to their door or something. Just use the language, call it what it is. There's nothing anyone can say that will make it worse." Nathaniel took his hands away from his face and Molly could see deep anguish in his face. "This is really embarrassing," he said. "I can't...there's no way to excuse what I've done. It's just that the pain was so intense, and I missed her so much."

"I think I understand."

"I thought I could just have another few weeks, you know, while I was on this trip, to keep her alive in my heart." His eyes were wet and Molly started to tear up.

"It must feel like a loss you'll never get over."

Nathaniel nodded, unable to speak. Molly reached for his hand and squeezed it, and tears flowed for both of them.

With effort, Nathaniel got control of himself. "I'm not sure if anyone has told you...we're all...the guests...getting ready to head back home. It's not that we haven't really enjoyed being here at La Baraque, and I want to thank you so much for your generosity and hospitality. But my boss at the hospital isn't the most understanding guy, and I'm afraid I might lose my job if I don't get back. And the others—I'm sure they'll be letting you know—they'll be leaving in the next few days as well."

Molly nodded, hiding her anxiety about the way her chance to catch the killer was slipping through her fingers.

"And please...let me apologize again for not being honest with you. I hope you understand that it was my own weakness that led me to pretend, not that I was trying to fool you or anything like that."

"Yes, Nathaniel. But I hope you can go home and face your sadness now. All those feelings—which are not weaknesses, not at all—are going to be waiting for you, you know? There's not really any way to make them go away except by feeling them."

"Thanks, Molly," he said, giving Molly's hand one more squeeze before leaving. "Just give a yell if you need anything." She stayed in bed, petting Bobo from time to time but mostly just looking out the window, waiting for the tingling in her arm to abate and her mind to clear.

❧

As the sun started to sink, the workers parked the excavator to one side and admired the hole, and then went to talk to Molly about the next week's schedule and what they hoped to accomplish if the weather held.

"Well, all that sounds wonderful," she said, managing a smile. She had been sitting by the woodstove flipping through a magazine.

"Guys, I'll catch up to you in a second," said Marc, the man in charge, and the two other men understood they were being dismissed and went out through the French doors.

Molly waited, expecting to be asked about when they would be paid or some detail about the pool she hadn't anticipated.

"It's probably nothing," Marc said. "But if there's anything I've learned in my life, it's not to ignore it when something catches your attention, you know?"

Molly waited, having no clue what he was talking about.

"So you know, we were hard at it most of the day. Took a break sometime in mid-afternoon. A drink from our thermoses, sit down, relax for a few minutes. And one of the tourists, a big guy, I see him come out of the woods a little ways toward the cottage. And right off I noticed something sort of...a little sneaky. Like he was looking to see if anyone was around, if anyone saw him. He was carrying a short shovel."

"Tall guy with shaggy blond hair? Big guy?"

"That's him, yeah. I kept my eye on him. He was looking all around and our eyes met, just for a moment. Then he hurried over to that little shed where I guess you keep gardening stuff? He stepped in there for a few moments and when he came back, he didn't have the shovel anymore."

"How odd," said Molly. "Sometimes my guests will ask to borrow this or that—tape, or ribbon, or a kitchen tool. But no one has ever asked for a shovel."

"Looked to me like he took it without asking. Like I say, he was looking...guilty."

Molly nodded. "Thanks, Marc. I definitely appreciate your telling me. I can't have my eyes on everyone all the time."

"No, madame."

After he took off, Molly went straight to the gardening shed. It wasn't as neat as she liked it to be—a bag of peat moss was spilling onto the floor, and several tools sat on a potting table instead of hanging on their rightful hooks on the wall. The short shovel (made, she thought, for digging holes for bulbs) had been in the shed when she bought La Baraque; she didn't think she had ever used it. It was leaning against the wall and she picked it up. The cutting edge of the blade was rimmed with dark, loamy dirt, which is what you would find in the forest if you pulled back the carpet of leaves.

She had no idea what Ira Bilson wanted to bury in the forest, but she intended to find out. Quickly she texted Ben to let him know where she was going. Then she whistled for Bobo, pulled a cap on her head, and walked down the length of the meadow toward the swimming pool, in case anyone from the cottage happened to be keeping a lookout. After observing the raw hole for the swimming pool for a while, she headed away from the forest and toward the old crumbling building she had talked to Pierre Gault about rebuilding. Seemed a lifetime ago, thought Molly.

She did not allow herself to get lost in old memories, however, but resolutely considered Ira Bilson and the shovel. Could he have buried the garrotte, knowing it would quickly disintegrate (if it was a cord made of cotton, the way she had always imagined)? Or perhaps he was burying drug paraphernalia, in preparation for the journey home and the inspection at customs?

Finally, after making sure she was not being followed, she moved into the forest. With a deep inhalation, she stood for a short moment taking it all in: the leafless branches barely moving overhead, the deep leaf litter, the quiet. She closed her eyes and was able to hear a small animal skittering nearby, and the peeping of a bird she could not identify. Bobo had long since streaked off chasing something or other, and so Molly made her way alone, scanning back and forth, looking for any disturbance on the forest floor. She was not a person with long experience in woodsmanship, but she guessed that if she was lucky enough to come across the place where Ira had used the shovel, she would be able to spot it.

And she was not wrong.

33

As a disappointed Molly emerged from the forest and into to the meadow at La Baraque, the Castillac police car was pulling into the driveway, and Maron quickly got out as Ben came out of the house to greet him. Did he have some news? Her muscles ached from the short walk, her arm still tingled, and heaven knew her brain was muddled. But Molly was not going to miss a meeting on the murder case no matter what.

"I...I hope my reliance on you is not causing any resentment," Maron said to Ben as they walked toward the house.

"I appreciate your forthrightness," said Ben, mildly surprised and pleased by the direct fashion in which his former protégé spoke to him. "It is no problem, and I very much hope we will be able to continue to work together once Molly and I get our private investigation business off the ground."

"I guess you'd have no opening with this case. It seems that no one is much interested in finding Pyke's murderer, other than us."

"The bureaucracy...it's always a disappointment, as I'm sure you know. And the man had no family."

"Isn't it a bit strange that someone as charismatic as Pyke—at least according to everyone at La Baraque—didn't have a group of friends back home yelling about this? I half expected to find an angry mob outside the gendarmerie as the days passed with no progress. Instead, nothing but silence. At any rate, I do have some news. Not as meaty as we might like, but it is something."

They came into the living room just as Molly entered through the French doors. They made their greetings and Molly sank gratefully into an armchair, exhausted. It had been a long day.

"All right then," said Maron, taking charge. "I have some background information to share with you. I do get the sense, from time to time, that law enforcement in Paris might know more than they are passing on, but eh, not much I can do about that. So. Let's focus for now on the couple, Ira and Darcy Bilson. Turns out they both have criminal records in America. Darcy has been convicted of shoplifting in several states. Never served time, but had to perform what they call 'community service.' Ira Bilson has gone to prison on a drug charge. Once there, he was punished multiple times for taking violent action against other inmates."

"Does that mean he got into fights? Or are you saying premeditated violence?" Molly asked.

"I can check back on that."

"It would be worth knowing," said Ben. "Shoplifting or drugs don't necessarily have much bearing on murder, but if Ira plotted to hurt someone in prison, that would be more relevant."

"Still, their behavior and records show a disregard for the law."

"I don't disagree. Though all we can do is use those facts to build a more complete picture of what kind of people they are. We can't consider it as evidence in our case."

"Of course not," snapped Maron.

"I was hoping to have something to add to our Bilson file," said Molly. "I'm having a pool put in, at the end of the meadow. One of the workmen saw Ira coming out the forest looking like he'd been up to something. He had a little shovel with him. So I ducked into the forest and wandered around looking to see if I could find what he had buried, since I checked the shovel and it did have fresh dirt on it."

Maron and Ben were leaning forward, eyebrows raised.

"Oh, don't look at me like that," said Molly, waving her hand at them. "Don't get your hopes up. I found the spot easily enough. He didn't make much effort to hide it. Well, any effort, really. I dug down with my hands and found a heap of food wrappers."

"Food wrappers?"

"Candy bars, chips, gummy worms...junk food. Seems a little bizarre, but then, we're not married to Darcy. I've heard her saying some mean things to Ira about his weight. Lately, he's been staying in when Darcy goes out, and I guess he's gone down to the *épicerie* for snacks when she's not looking. Maybe he figured if he got rid of the evidence that way, he'd avoid some of her barbs."

Ben just shook his head. "Some marriages are a total mystery to me."

"Did you look inside the wrappers?" asked Maron.

"Yes, Gilles. I had visions of finding the garrotte tucked inside a Haribo bag. No luck. Of course, feel free to send a forensics person out if you'd like, but I combed through it all carefully. It was just trash."

"A shame. Well, I'm going to question Ira anyway. He's in the cottage? I'll stop back by if I find out anything worth sharing."

Maron let himself out and Ben put some water on for tea. "Well, that was interesting, if not terribly helpful. Now, back to bed with you," he said. "I'll bring the green tea in as soon as it's ready. Anything else Dr. Vernay say you should be taking?"

Molly sighed and made no move to get up. "I'm so sick of being sick," she said.

"Of course you are." He paused a moment, then asked, "Do *you* think it's Ira?"

"I wish I knew. I'll tell you though, I thought I had the Bilsons pegged. There's a type back home, city people who decide they want to farm or lead some kind of country life, but they've still got a city temperament."

"You mean difficult?"

"Right. 'Testy,' we call it in English. A little defensive, a bit aggressive maybe. Quick to take offense. But not druggie shoplifters, you know? Anyway, I admired them for having this dream of a herd of goats and making good cheese. It's nice to have ambitions, and that seemed like a fine one to me."

"Doesn't exactly match with their criminal histories, does it?"

"No. But I guess I'm just being shallow and judgmental. People can change, right? No reason why a former shoplifter couldn't be a perfectly good goat herd."

Ben shrugged.

"You'd think I'd have learned by now that people aren't always who they seem to be on the surface. Ryan...."

"Pyke."

"Yes, I mean Pyke. The charming serial embezzler." Molly slowly shook her head. "Maybe I should start running record checks on my guests before taking any reservations," she said with a laugh, but it was a laugh of disbelief more than mirth.

❧

MOLLY HAD FORGOTTEN that she had an appointment with Dr. Vernay until Lawrence arrived to take her.

"Oh, gracious!" she said, when she opened the door. "Totally forgot! Can you wait two minutes for me to...." she pointed at her hair, which looked a little like Medusa's with red curly snakes flying out from all angles.

"I'm a smidgen early," said Lawrence. "Do you have your notes ready?"

"Notes?"

"Do I not remember that Dr. Vernay asked you to keep a record of your symptoms from day to day?"

"Oh."

"Molly!"

"I know. I just...now that you mention it, I remember him saying that. But it flew right out of my head just as soon as I left his office. I didn't even make one entry."

"Oh well, he won't yell at you for too long."

"Lawrence!"

"Kidding, my dear, kidding."

They arrived at Dr. Vernay's office with a few minutes to spare.

"Bonjour, Molly!" said Robinette, the doctor's wife. "Ah, I see you're not feeling well. I will let the doctor know you are here."

"Does she have to say things like that?" whispered Molly to Lawrence after she stepped into the other room. "Do I look that bad?"

Lawrence took a moment to appraise his friend. "You are, unbelievably, paler than usual. There are dark bags under your eyes that you normally do not have. Your hair—"

"Never mind!"

"So tell me about the case. What progress have you made?"

Molly shrugged. "More or less zero. I think we're all pretty much in agreement that it was probably Ira Bilson who killed Pyke, out of jealousy. Though you would think he might be happy to think another man might take his wife away from him."

Lawrence chuckled. "Not a charming woman?"

"A *long* way from charming. Anyway, Bilson served time and has a record of violence. But of course, none of that is proof. Without the murder weapon or some kind of forensic evidence, we've got no way to charge him, or even keep him here in France any longer."

"Is this going to be the case that finally eludes you?"

"Oh, don't put it like that. It's not like I have some illustrious career. And who knows, maybe something will eventually come to light, and we can go after him then."

"Or maybe the killer will turn out to be someone else altogether."

Molly whipped her gaze toward him. "Do you know something?"

"No, no. Simply musing, chérie."

The examination with Dr. Vernay went smoothly enough. He gave Molly a little notebook in which to record her symptoms and did not yell at her at all. She was also grateful to hear that he judged her recovery was coming along as he'd expected.

"Be well! Those eye bags will disappear eventually, no doubt!" Robinette said in farewell, and Molly managed to smile and wave goodbye, and not say what she was thinking.

34

Ben was making omelets and a green salad for him and Molly to have for dinner. He uncorked a rather nice red wine, feeling a little guilty since Molly was abstaining from alcohol during her recovery (except for that one slip with a kir). Bobo trotted back and forth from bedroom to kitchen, disturbed that her two humans weren't in the same room.

A quick rap on the French door, and Maron let himself in.

"Mon Dieu," he muttered. "I just finished with Ira Bilson. He had quite a bit more to say than I had expected."

"Let me see if Molly can join us," said Ben, quickly sliding the second omelet onto a plate and hurrying into the bedroom. He returned with a disheveled but conscious Molly.

"I was just dreaming about the case," she said, her cheeks flushed. "It's maybe the third dream I've had about this woman lying on her back, with really pale skin. No, it's not me," she said to Ben's inquiring expression. "No idea why I keep dreaming about a dead woman when it's a man who got strangled."

Maron was not interested in Molly's dreams. "I put some pressure on Bilson," he said. "Which to my surprise, he told me he was expecting. 'You have a prison record and somebody gets murdered, you know the cops will be headed your way' is what he told me. Figured we'd get around to suspecting him sooner or later. So, for his own defense, he's been spending his time digging up dirt on all the other guests."

"How resourceful," Ben said.

"Can't wait to hear what he found. But first, Gilles, are you hungry? Want Ben to make you an omelet? He's very good at it."

"I'm sure. No, thank you. I want to tell you what Ira told me, and get home. Go ahead and eat while we talk, I don't mind."

Molly and Ben sat on stools at the counter and dug into their dinner. Molly looked at the wine longingly, but did not give in.

"It's sort of amazing what one can find online if one knows how to look," said Maron. "Of course, we'll need to do some verification, but on the face of it, it seems as though Bilson knows his way around a computer. He could be making it all up, but I doubt it—and he puts the 'experts' in the States and in Paris to shame.

All right, for the biggest bombshell, let's start with Ashley Gander. Apparently, she did not actually attend Auburn University. Not only does she not have a degree, she was never admitted. During my interview with her, she told me that she had met Patty McMahon while they were something called 'sorority sisters' at Auburn University in Alabama. You will understand this better than I, Molly—it's an American thing, this sorority?"

"Yes, a sorority is a club that college women join. Usually there are a number of them at a school. They might be competitive to get into or not. Lots of parties and rituals. But you have to actually be enrolled in school to join one, as far as I know. You can't just wander in off the streets."

"Well, then either she and Patty are lying about how they met—which seems like a curious lie, since who would care?—or Ashley faked her way into the sorority by pretending to be a student. Ira was adamant that she has never had any actual connection to Auburn at all."

"So, a rather grand liar. The hallmark of a sociopath, by the way," said Ben.

"Oh, and that's not all," said Maron, allowing himself to smile broadly. "Bilson found evidence—which he showed me on his laptop—that Ashley Gander was once the girlfriend of Ryan Tuck."

Ben and Molly sat stunned.

"Girlfriend?" she finally croaked. "Not of Pyke, but *Tuck?* But...."

A long silence.

"That makes no sense," said Ben.

Silence, as all three detectives approached the new fact from different angles, trying to fit it into a narrative, any narrative. "Well," said Molly slowly. "Maybe she found out Ryan was coming here, somehow, and wanted to get back together with him? Or confront him?"

"Or kill him," muttered Maron.

"But if she wanted to kill Ryan, she wouldn't have gone ahead and murdered someone else traveling under Ryan's name. And just to add another layer of weirdness: she *really* fell for Pyke. How likely is it that someone gets a crush on a man impersonating a former boyfriend?"

All Maron and Ben could do was shake their heads.

"Did Ira find out who broke up with whom?"

"He did not say, but you are right to ask the question. I did not think of it," said Maron sheepishly.

"And why did Ashley not say anything when she first saw that it was not the real Ryan Tuck?"

"Perhaps the plan to meet him was a secret, even to Patty, and so accusing Pyke of impersonating Ryan would have exposed her plan?"

Molly nodded slowly, thinking. "Wow. I wonder...I'm thinking Patty's going to be stunned to hear this. Is there any way she was in on it somehow? But what on earth would be her motive?"

"I knocked on Ashley's door before coming here, but there was no answer. Believe me, I'll be asking some of these questions as soon as I get hold of her. Now, Patty McMahon. Yes, well. She's got problems of her own. Patty's mother, Rebecca McMahon, was arrested for child abuse twelve years ago. She had a good lawyer and ended up getting off on some sort of technicality. Ira says it was all over the local news at the time."

"Whoa. Was it Patty she was abusing?"

"According to Bilson, it was a younger brother. He was kept in a closet for several months because he was caught looking at something called a Victoria's Secret catalog?"

Molly laughed. "It's for underwear. I'm laughing because these days, an underwear catalog is pretty tame. The models have clothes on, even if skimpy ones." She ate a mouthful of omelet. "I'm not laughing about the abuse. Poor kid. Do you know what happened to him? Or whether Patty was involved in any way?"

"The arrest took place after Patty had left for college. Though it would be unexpected, wouldn't you say, for the mother to have been fine before that one incident? Who knows what she might have been up to before that she *wasn't* caught doing. She may also have abused Patty, for all we know."

"Okay, we've got one seriously dysfunctional family, a shoplifter, a felon, and a major league liar. How about Nathaniel? What horrors is he keeping under wraps?" said Molly, not quite joking, and fearing what Maron might say.

"Bilson said he hit a brick wall with Monsieur Beech. Could find almost no proof of his existence at all—only his name as an employee of the hospital where he told me he works, so at least that checks out. Bilson did say that it is not unusual for a person who works in IT to have a strict policy about privacy. It's the rest of us who blithely leave our online doors and windows open for all the world to see, so to speak."

❧

BEN LEFT EARLY the next morning, taking the TGV up to Paris to meet with his contacts, though they did not promise to have any earth-shattering developments to relate. Molly made herself breakfast, and then snuggled under a throw by the woodstove. She sat for a few hours, thinking about Jim Pyke, and about the secrets everyone keeps. It was deeply dispiriting for a murder to have taken place practically in her backyard, yet so far, have been incapable of solving it. For the first time, she was on the verge of calling it a loss and moving on. One thing was certain: she was not enjoying this first taste of failure.

All the guests were preparing to head back to the States in the next few days. Maron had hoped that one of them would try to bolt early out of fear of being caught, but that had not happened, and as far as holding them any longer, he was powerless in the absence of any hard evidence. In a way, they were as tight a group now as they had been in those first, innocent days. That night they were all going to a fancy restaurant in Bergerac to celebrate the end of their time in France. Perhaps one of them was also celebrating getting away with murder.

Molly wondered if any of them would ever come back. And of course, she wondered if it was really true that one of the five had committed the murder after all. It was painful to think that she might never know, that someone might be getting away with killing Ryan. Well, Jim. Her brain still violently resisted accepting that the man she had gotten to know—or thought she knew—was an imposter.

Okay, he *was* an embezzler, and probably a cad. But Pyke had thrown sticks for Bobo, and Molly had not forgotten that. Or his passion for gougères. He might have been generally no good, but even so, he hadn't been *all* bad. At the very least, he deserved the justice of his killer being caught and imprisoned. And what a motley gang the rest of the guests had turned out to be! Had it simply been a crazy bit of bad luck to get so many visitors with dark histories, all the same week? From the outside, they seemed like any group of somewhat befuddled tourists. A blue-ribbon group for February 2007, that's for sure.

But maybe, she thought a little more generously, maybe that's just humanity for you. All of us with warts of some kind or other, all of us with chapters in our lives we'd rather no one read.

A light tap on the French door and Molly saw Nathaniel waving to her. She gestured for him to come inside. "Hey Molly," he said. "I've decided to stay here instead of going out with everyone tonight, so I wanted to ask—"

"Natha—"

"I know, you'll tell me to go with them! But look, you're not well, and I just wouldn't feel right leaving you here by yourself. Ben is away, right?"

"Yes, but—"

"And it's not just that. I'm feeling sort of worn down by this whole vacation. It hasn't done much to help me get over Miranda after all. Maybe you don't just 'get over' the death of a fiancée. So, you know, I'm not really in the mood to go out anyway. I'll just kill two birds with one stone by being available to give you help if you need it. You could use a man around the house, feeling as poorly as you do."

"Honestly, I'm not that bad off. Go, have fun! Who knows when you'll come back to France, Nathaniel."

"You're not going to talk me into it, Molly," he said, his eyes bright. "Anything you need now?" He came closer, taking her hands and looking at her with intensity.

She caught a faint whiff of something and her head jerked. What was that? A faint scent of...?

"No, please, don't worry about me."

"All right then, I'll be reading in my room. Just text me, I'm two steps away if you need me."

Molly sighed, having nowhere near enough energy to argue. "All right. I hope you enjoy your quiet evening. I don't expect to need anything. I'm fine, really."

Nathaniel saluted and went back out through the French doors. Molly sat for a while longer, trying to remember where she had smelled that scent before. It was so fleeting, so hard to hold onto. She wondered if anyone was going to tell Patty about Ashley's lies, and whether their friendship would survive. And what about the Bilsons? Would they ever get their herd of goats? With a wry smile, she thought she would not suggest a reunion...if any of them wanted to see each other again, let them go to Provence next time. Or Australia. Someplace comfortably far from Castillac.

The fire was burning down, but the effort it would take to go outside for more wood was daunting, and Nathaniel was probably back in his room already. Molly called Bobo and went back to bed, pulling the comforter up to her chin and getting warm that way. The orange cat came in and walked over her still body, and before long, she was once again asleep.

35

She was lying on her phone when it started buzzing. Very slowly and with great effort, Molly dragged herself awake, blinking her eyes hard and licking her dry lips, barely managing to answer the phone in time.

"I'm glad to hear you're resting," Ben said gently.

"I'm awake! Really," she said, unconvincingly. She could hear the sounds of Paris traffic in the background.

"Why do people always say that," Ben said, and she could hear the smile in his voice. "It's not like being asleep is a crime. Especially when Dr. Vernay has said to get as much of it as possible."

Molly made a grumbling noise but did not answer.

"Okay then, I've had two different meetings on two different park benches," said Ben. "The Luxembourg Gardens are quite lovely this time of year. Stark, but beautiful."

Molly lay back down and closed her eyes, trying to picture what Ben was describing.

"I'm afraid we're boxed in by brick walls every way we turn," he continued. "As my friend warned me, he didn't have anything helpful. He's been working on the Ryan Tuck angle, trying to determine if he was the actual target of the murder. Piece of work, that Ryan."

Ben said something garbled that Molly couldn't make out.

"Ben? This connection is terrible. What did you just say?"

"I said, apparently his modus operandi is to move all over the country, preying on trusting women and conning them out of their money, or at least convincing them to support him for extended lengths of time. Inevitably they figure out what he's up to and throw him out. Or sue him. According to his sister, he regularly crawls back to their hometown and hides out while the latest brouhaha blows over. At the moment he's living in a trailer on someone else's property and doesn't even have a phone. The guy seems to have figured out pretty well how to make himself untraceable."

"It's a big country," said Molly.

"Indeed." Ben continued to speak but the static blotted out half of his words. "The sister was going on and on about how he owes her money—*xxxzzzxxpp*"

"What? Did you say Ryan owes his sister money?"

"*xxxxzzz*...and he'd actually gotten a bequest, insurance money *xxxzzzxxx* Miranda Cunningh—*xxxzzzzz*—"

Molly snapped all the way awake. "What? Say that again?"

"*Xzzzz*"

"Ben!"

The call dropped. Frantically she called right back.

"Sorry!" he said. "Our connection—*xxzzz*"

"Did you say Miranda Cunningham was a girlfriend of Ryan Tuck's?" Molly jumped out of bed, her heart racing.

But the call dropped again, and the line was dead.

In the next instant, it all came back. It was Nathaniel's cologne that she had smelled in Pyke's room the morning he was killed.

I am the biggest sucker in the world, she thought. And her next thought was that she had better hustle over to her neighbor's right away. Before she could pull herself together, a firm rap on her bedroom door.

"Just a minute!" she called out, trying to keep her voice confident. Should she duck out the window? Calm down, Molly, she told herself. He's not going to hurt you. But she was not calm. The lies had been thick and she had been utterly fooled. But at long last she was starting to see the truth, or something close enough.

Frozen, she watched with dread as the door opened slowly.

"Molls?" he said. "Oh, look at you, up and out of bed. I hope that's a sign you're feeling better!"

Molly wanted to avoid eye contact, as though he would see that she knew if their eyes met, but she understood it was imperative to act as naturally as possible. "Well, I *am* feeling better. I just wish...."

"What? Shall I draw you a bath? Make you something to eat?"

"You're too kind, Nathaniel. You'll make some lucky woman a good husband someday." God, don't strike me down for lying just now, she prayed. "I may have mentioned—what's funny about this illness is how it messes with my taste buds. A lot of things just don't taste right."

"Are you craving something in particular, is that it? You're not pregnant, are you?"

She knew he was only trying to joke with her but the remark made her want to slap him. "No, not pregnant," she answered lightly. "But I would so love to have a box of those mini-toasts you only see in France. Have you had them? They are absolutely delicious. Especially with goat cheese, as Darcy may have mentioned."

Nathaniel laughed. "I pretty much tune her out when she starts going on about cheese. Okay, where can I get this magical toast?"

"The épicerie in the village always has them. Would you really go? You don't mind?"

"I skipped the fancy dinner just to take care of you," he said. "Of course I'll go. I'm happy to. The shop is right up the street from the Café de la Place, have I got it right?"

"That's it. Thank you so much! I really appreciate it."

Nathaniel smiled and bowed awkwardly, and left the bedroom. Molly snatched up her phone and tried to call Ben again, but what he could he do, all the way in Paris?

Calm down, Molly, she thought to herself. It will take him at least twenty minutes to get those toasts, and that's if he jogs all the way there and back. She had a flash of Pyke, hanging in the forest, his arms dangling down. Molly shuddered.

When Nathaniel gets to the épicerie, he'll see that it closed hours ago, and he'll realize I've sent him on a wild goose chase.

She called Maron and left a message when he did not answer, and put on her coat. She was not quite panicked thanks to the twenty-minute window, but as she tried to gather her things and leave, she was hobbled by an inability to think clearly.

I should take a handbag.

Where is my phone?

Ben did say Miranda Cunningham, didn't he? Could the bad connection have made me hear the wrong thing?

What else do I need?

Molly stood in the corridor, trying to think. It didn't matter whether she took a bag, the point was to leave and leave now.

But no sooner had Molly finally grasped that bit of truth than she heard footsteps just outside the front door.

"Oh, Molly," said Nathaniel sadly, as he stepped inside. "I was getting onto the road on the way to the store, when I realized—it's Sunday evening and everything will be closed. Isn't that right?"

With a classic deer-in-the-headlights expression, Molly managed a forced smile. "Oh, I suppose you're right. Sometimes I forget I don't live in Boston anymore, where there is almost always someplace open. Plus I'm so forgetful lately." She watched his face. For the first time, Molly was uncomfortable in

Nathaniel's presence. Intensely so. The young man leaned in her direction, watchful, and she felt as though he wanted to flood her with his feelings, all of the emotion he held inside, a tidal wave of hurt and anguish.

She had no plan. All she could do was stall while she tried to think of something.

"How about we go in the living room for a while and talk? Would you mind bringing in just an armful of wood? It's right around the corner of the house. Would you like a cup of hot chocolate? I think I can find a box of cocoa somewhere, and yesterday Monsieur Cherac from down the road brought me some milk from his famous Normande cows."

"Wonderful! If you're up to making it?"

"Of course." She glanced over and saw him savagely picking at his cuticles. "Did you love hot chocolate when you were a kid?"

"We hardly ever had it."

"What? Now that is close to criminal. I will always give my mother credit for doing an excellent job in the kitchen. She would go on these jags every so often—she'd cook Russian food for a month, or Thai. That was before you could get Thai food all over. What's your favorite kind of food?"

Nathaniel looked disconcerted by her chatter. He did not answer but got up from the stool and began to pace. "You should get back in bed. The others will be back soon," he said.

"Oh no, a dinner like that goes on for hours. You wouldn't believe all the courses," said Molly, wanting him to be at ease and also praying they came back far earlier than she dared hope. "So, it's a little chilly in here, don't you think? You wouldn't mind getting the wood?"

Nathaniel went distractedly through the French doors, and Molly pulled out her cell and opened her contacts, looking for the number at the station where possibly Paul-Henri would be on duty. But before she could find it, Nathaniel was back, and looking at her strangely. Was he distrustful? Angry? Molly tried to read his expression but could not. He was obviously distressed. And on top of that, his actions seemed dangerously unpredictable.

Molly watched as he knelt by the woodstove and jammed in a fresh log, then another one. Quietly she stirred the milk while it heated, then whisked in heaping spoonfuls of cocoa and sugar while Nathaniel put more logs in the stove and fiddled with the air intake. When the cocoa was hot, Molly filled two mugs and brought them over.

"Here you are," she said. "I'm just going to...sit down for a moment. There."

"You shouldn't be up. I told you that you should be resting." He stood up, turning his back to her and looking out of the window into the darkness. For a long moment he said nothing, and then his words came in a rush. "I just want you to understand. You don't know what it's like. You don't know how much I want to help, how much I want to fix it."

Molly stayed silent.

"And Miranda...she's so much like you. When I went to meet her that day, I was totally bowled over by the resemblance. And it wasn't just the sickness, either. She had a kind of...of serenity, I guess, that reminded me of you. I was very drawn to her because of that. Serenity—" he laughed harshly, "—I don't have a lot of that in my life. Not since...."

Molly held her breath. She followed his lead—bowing her head as though too fatigued to hold it up. Finally she lifted her eyes just enough to meet his in the reflection in the window. "Yes," she said faintly. "You take such good care of me."

Nathaniel kept his back turned. He has to do that to maintain the fantasy, Molly thought. If he looks right at me, he can't pretend, it falls apart....

"If you would please talk to me, Nathaniel," she said, hoping to hit on something his mother might have said to him. "Tell me about your life. I don't have the strength to have a real conversation, but I would very much like to hear about *you*."

Without looking at her face, he turned and handed her a blanket. She tucked it around herself and settled back into the chair, looking as weak and frail as she could, and at the same time, somehow maternal. Molly allowed herself a small moan, imagining herself wracked with pain from a terrible cancer.

"I kept coming back to visit with Miranda, even after the administrative problem had long since been dealt with. She was very beautiful, you know. There can be a beauty in illness. I want you to know that."

"Thank you, my dear," Molly murmured.

"Some days she was too sick to see me, and I hated being turned away like that. The nurse told me not to take it personally, but that's a pretty tall order when being with someone is that important to you. When it's your whole life, really."

"You love Miranda."

"Yes! That's the most important thing about all of this. That's what I want you especially to understand. It's all out of love for her." He flashed Molly a quick smile then looked away again. "On her better days, I would sneak out of my cubicle and sit with her for hours. She talked and talked. I heard the whole story of her life, about how it was before she got sick." He turned suddenly and glowered at Molly. "She told me about Ryan Tuck," he said, the words dripping with contempt.

When he said Ryan's name, Molly felt a deadly chill course through her body despite the roaring woodstove. She didn't dare say a word.

"Ryan Tuck was all fun and games—with *her* money—until the cancer diagnosis. Then he took off. Can you even believe it? Your girlfriend gets desperately sick with something that can kill her, and you pick that moment to bail on her? And the crazy thing, the really crazy thing?" Nathaniel's chin dropped to his chest.

Molly heard a gurgling, choking sound as he tried to stop himself from breaking down.

"She still missed him?" Molly said softly.

"Yes. She still missed him. I could not *believe* it. I told her she was worth a hundred Ryan Tucks, that she was way too good for the likes of him. But you know, that did not give her any comfort at all. It was better if we talked about something else."

A long moment passed in silence. Molly stayed still in the armchair, straining to hear Christophe's taxi in the driveway bringing the other guests home.

"I think the stove could take another log," she said, fearing what he might be thinking about and wanting to keep him busy.

"Anything I can do for you, Mom," said Nathaniel. "You know I'll do anything."

Molly froze. He did not appear to have heard the slip of the tongue. Maybe I have a chance, she thought.

"But you fixed it, didn't you?" she said, making her voice reedy and thin.

"Well, I tried. I tried! Tuck is a little sneak and after he ran off no one could find him. But I did! Or at least, I found that a Ryan Tuck had signed up for a week's vacation here at La Baraque. You have that little chat area on your website, for guests to leave comments and questions? For weeks I could find no internet presence at all. I did some massive searches, I used every trick in the book to try and find him, and ended up at your website. I was pretty proud of myself for that."

"Only the person leaving that message was Jim Pyke. And it wasn't until the gendarme informed everyone that the man who came to La Baraque wasn't really Ryan Tuck...."

"How was I supposed to know?" he said mournfully. "I was only trying to avenge Miranda's death. She...I won't say she died of a broken heart, because the cancer killed her sure enough. But she died *with* a broken heart, I can say that much. And Ryan Tuck

—he pretty much gave her a big shove right into the grave, abandoning her like he did."

"You stood up for her."

"Who else did she have on her side? Nobody. Not one other person ever came to the hospital, and she was there for six whole weeks."

"I'm so sorry, Nathaniel," Molly said carefully. She sneaked a peek at her phone to see the time. The others might not be back for another hour. Ben was probably still on the TGV, or even spending another night in Paris.

Molly decided to take the biggest risk of her young investigative career. "Shall I call the gendarme?" she asked, as simply as though she were asking whether he wanted ketchup on his hamburger.

"Might as well," Nathaniel said, his voice cracking. The young man lowered his lanky body onto the arm of the chair where Molly sat, put his arms around her, and sobbed into her neck.

EPILOGUE

"Wait, wait, wait," Lawrence was saying to Molly over the din at Chez Papa. "You're saying the guy actually thought you were his dead mother? How in hell did you pull that one off?"

"It wasn't exactly like that. I mean, if you had pointed at me and asked him point blank, is this your mother? I'm fairly sure he'd have said no, how dare you—that's Molly. It was more like... Nathaniel lived in a kind of murky emotional place where the edges and boundaries got blurry sometimes. Does that make any sense?"

"Not really," chimed in Ben, taking a sip from a large glass of red wine and then setting it back on the bar. "He did call you Mom, right?"

"Yes, but...look, he was talking to his mother *through* me, in a way. I helped him feel close to her again, almost as though she wasn't entirely gone. I know, it seems crazy. It *is* crazy. But to me anyway, it does make a kind of sense. His dreams of what he wished to happen occasionally got a little confused with what was actually happening."

"And he was never the boyfriend of this Miranda Cunningham at all?" asked Lawrence.

"Correct," said Ben. "He worked at the hospital, and nurses have given testimony that he did visit her a great deal. But Miranda was desperately ill. Dying, actually. Hardly in any shape to be starting a relationship, even if she had wanted to."

"And he came all the way to France to get revenge on her behalf. Now that's what I call chivalry," said Lawrence.

"I think it got mixed up in his head with saving his mother somehow," said Molly.

"We were so focused on Jim Pyke being the intended victim," Ben said to Lawrence, "but poor Monsieur Beech killed him thinking he was Ryan Tuck."

"Everything was about Tuck, in the end. One of the guests, Ashley Gander, had been with Tuck a couple of years ago. They had a tempestuous relationship apparently, and split up, but Ashley recently broke up with someone else and got curious about what Tuck was up to. She found him in the comments section of my website too, same as Nathaniel had. So she booked a reservation, and then talked her old friend Patty into coming to hide the fact that she was stalking him."

"Must have been something of a shock to find another man using Tuck's name."

"Eh, one thing about Ashley? She adapts quickly," laughed Molly.

"How did the other guests react to the news about Nathaniel?" asked Ben.

Molly laughed. "It was a zoo, as you might expect. Ira was deeply relieved, and for good reason, since we had all painted a target on him. Ashley was running around crowing that she had known all along and why hadn't anyone listened to her. Darcy, to her credit, seemed happy for Ira. The only one who didn't receive the news with glee was Patty, who had spent more time alone with Nathaniel than anyone else and considered him a friend, I believe.

Anyway, they've all left now. The Bilsons missed a connection at Orly so they're still in France, but the others are safely back in the good ol' USA by now."

"Whew," said Lawrence.

"You said it!" said Molly.

"I was thinking..." said Ben to her, "maybe we should go on a little vacation—just the two of us? Maybe in another month, when you'll be done with your Lyme treatments and feeling better?"

"Where?" asked Molly, loving the idea.

"The Maldives?" said Lawrence. "Morocco is always nice."

"How about Italy?" asked Ben, not having considered Italy before that moment.

"Perfect," said Molly. "But let's not wait a month. I feel fine, I really do. In fact, as soon as I finish my kir, I'm going to go home and pack. Let's take the next flight."

Lawrence and Ben cracked up laughing and ordered another round of drinks. Molly was back, the killer had been caught, and at least for that moment, all was right in the village of Castillac.

THE END

ALSO BY NELL GODDIN

The Third Girl (Molly Sutton Mysteries 1)

The Luckiest Woman Ever (Molly Sutton Mysteries 2)

The Prisoner of Castillac (Molly Sutton Mysteries 3)

Murder for Love (Molly Sutton Mysteries 4)

The Château Murder (Molly Sutton Mysteries 5)

Murder on Vacation (Molly Sutton Mysteries 6)

An Official Killing (Molly Sutton Mysteries 7)

Death in Darkness (Molly Sutton Mysteries 8)

No Honor Among Thieves (Molly Sutton Mysteries 9)

GLOSSARY

1:

La Baraque............the house or shed
gîte.......................holiday cottage for rent, usually by the week
gendarmes..............police
frites.....................French fries
pain au chocolat.......croissant with a chocolate center

2:

pâtisserie..............pastry shop
département..........county

3:

pigeonnier...........dovecote (in this case, remodeled into a gîte)
gougères.............cheesy puffs

bienvenue............welcome
à tout à l'heure......see you later

4:

priez pour vos morts......pray for your dead
gendarmerie................police station

5:

Castillaçois...............people who live in Castillac

9:

coup de foudre.........lightning bolt

11:

chérie....................dear
traiteur.................caterer

15:

Allô...................hello (on telephone)

18:

Mon Dieu.............My God

20:

cabécou................kind of cheese

. . .

24:

sablés..................shortbread cookies

33:

épicerie................small grocery store

ACKNOWLEDGMENTS

Bountiful thanks to Tommy Glass for his impeccable word-polishing and plotting support, and to Nancy Kelley for her very valuable insights and unfailing honesty.

Also big thanks to Michelle Lowery, who is the best proof-reader ever.

ABOUT THE AUTHOR

Nell Goddin has worked as a radio reporter, SAT tutor, short-order omelet chef, and baker. She tried waitressing but was fired twice.

Nell grew up in Richmond, Virginia and has lived in New England, New York City, and France. Currently she's back in Virginia with teenagers and far too many pets. She has degrees from Dartmouth College and Columbia University.

www.nellgoddin.com
nell@nellgoddin.com

Made in the USA
Coppell, TX
27 August 2024

36503719R10152